A STREAK OF LIGHTNING

Warlocks MacGregor®

MICHELLE M. PILLOW

MichellePillow.com

A Streak of Lightning (*Warlocks MacGregor*®) © copyright 2022 by Michelle M. Pillow

First Printing July 26, 2022

ISBN: 978-1-62501-320-0

Published by The Raven Books LLC

ALL RIGHTS RESERVED.

All books copyrighted to the author and may not be resold or given away without written permission from the author, Michelle M. Pillow.

This novel is a work of fiction. Any and all characters, events, and places are of the author's imagination and should not be confused with fact. Any resemblance to persons, living or dead, or events or places is merely coincidence. Novel intended for adults only. Must be 18 years or older to read.

Michelle M. Pillow® and *Warlocks MacGregor*® are registered trademarks of The Raven Books LLC

About A Streak of Lightning

A modern-day Scottish paranormal romance by NYT Bestselling Author Michelle M. Pillow.

Lightning isn't the only thing streaking in small-town Wisconsin.

Warlock Raibeart MacGregor is on the prowl and looking for his true love. He has only one question for any lassie he meets, "Will ya marry me?" With his sanity often questioned by those who know him best, Raibeart believes there is a method to his madness. At least he hopes so. He's convinced his true love exists, but he just can't seem to find her.

Plagued by nightmares, he's compelled to run himself to exhaustion each night to keep them at bay. The fact that he prefers to drop the kilt while doing so is just a bonus. But when those nightmares begin to bleed into reality, he realizes the woman he's been searching for is literally the one tormenting his dreams.

Katherine Galbraith has been imprisoned by magick for so long that she can't even remember what her crime was beyond the vague impression that she once loved a warlock. Bound to a world that never changes, she spends her days wishing for an end. But when prison walls begin to crack, she must decide if she wants a second chance at lost love or if that love is the reason for all her suffering.

Magic, Mischief and Kilts!

Warlocks MacGregor® Series

SCOTTISH MAGICKAL WARLOCKS

Love Potions
Spellbound
Stirring Up Trouble
Cauldrons and Confessions
Spirits and Spells
Kisses and Curses
Magick and Mischief
A Dash of Destiny
Night Magick
A Streak of Lightning
Magickal Trouble

More Coming Soon

Visit www.MichellePillow.com for details.

Author Updates

Join the Reader Club Mailing List to stay informed about new books, sales, contests and preorders!

http://michellepillow.com/author-updates/

Note from the Author

The term "warlock" is a variation on the Old English word "waerloga" primarily used by the Scots. It meant traitor, monster, deceiver, or other variations. The MacGregors do not look at themselves as being what history has labeled their kind. To them, warlock means magick, family, and immortality. This book is not meant to be a portrayal of modern day witches or those who have such beliefs. The MacGregors are a magickal class all their own.

As with all my books, this is pure fantasy. In real life, please always practice safe sex and magic(k).

To The Pillow Fighter Fan Club
This one is for you lassies!

Chapter One

How could she escape a prison without walls?

Katherine stood inside her small world, contained within shadows and sand. Each day poured over her like tiny grains, dropping one by one onto her head, so insignificant they hardly seemed to matter, and yet, laid around her feet, they created the land on which she walked. This eternal trap was her price to pay for having loved a warlock.

She was a pet, some animal caged within invisible walls. If she walked along the beach, near the raging oceans, and kept walking, she would come back around to her own footprints but never a barrier. She'd pass the same small cottage and hear the same bleating from an invisible goat.

Around and around, she'd walk until she found herself too exhausted to go on. Then she would sleep, tormented by nightmares of her past, little glimpses that faded during the waking hours. No matter where she collapsed, she awoke in the same bed.

There was one torment in the prison worse than the rest, a mirror in which she did not see her reflection. Within it, she received short glimpses into the world beyond. At first, she had stood transfixed before it. She watched her parents and siblings age and die, their lives so brief and long ago that she now struggled to remember what they looked like. She watched the landscape change from untamed prairies to strange upright buildings, from carts to contraptions to these strange containers that did not need horses.

There had been other things, worse things, that were too hard to bear watching. They had broken her heart over and over again until the ache became a permanent fixture in her chest, even when she couldn't remember what they were.

Food appeared at her wooden table, the variety losing all charm after countless days. If she broke all the furniture, set fire to the cottage, or threw the food at the wall, her mess would right itself the moment she closed her eyes to sleep.

When her rage had been spent, she'd find herself on a cliff over the water. It would seem the only reason for its existence was to tease her into jumping. Katherine had not wanted to end her life before this prison. She'd been taught that each day was precious. Undoubtedly, that sentiment was held by those who didn't face immortality.

Death never claimed her.

She had jumped and felt her body crash against the cliffs. She'd hung herself from the rafters. She'd dug a hole and buried herself alive. She had stabbed herself with shards from the mirror, burned herself, starved herself, and drowned herself in the ocean. Each time, desperate and suffering and feeling each dying breath, she hoped it would be the last. But then she woke up in the same damned bed with its red covers.

Katherine knew this world. She'd counted each stone, knew each brush of unchanging plaster, and had stared at the grains in the wood until each was like a friend, and so it stood to reason that the tiny fracture along the wall would catch her attention. When she stood close, it stretched before her like a dry riverbed, running from ceiling to floor.

Where had this crack come from?

Katherine stared at the change, afraid that if she looked away the hallucination would right itself. She tried not to allow herself to hope that this crack signaled the beginning of the end and that she would finally find eternal rest.

Chapter Two

Pinecones on a bare ass were no way to start a night.

Raibeart MacGregor burrowed in hiding between two trunks. The still evening air did not stir the leaves of the surrounding forest. The sound of their rustling came from the little creatures who jumped from branch to branch overhead. As rays of moonlight made their way through the treetops to dance across his naked body, he didn't bother to wonder where he'd left his kilt. The thing always showed up in the morning. He'd enchanted it so he'd stop losing his favorite clothes.

The women in his family always fussed about his running around at night in his birthday suit. Then again, women seemed to enjoy making fusses about things. Who was he to deny them that pleasure? He liked to see the womenfolk happy.

Back in the day, some of his Viking friends used to charge into battle naked, their swords erect and their man bits dangling for the world to see. At least he wasn't fighting anyone on his nightly jaunts to exhaustion.

Raibeart checked the tiny claw marks along his thigh. Gremians didn't count. The feisty little arseholes had ambushed him as he'd entered the wooded path on the MacGregor property for his nightly run. Now they hunted him. He heard the pack of gnarled little goblins jumping back and forth, scouting the forest for his movements.

The family property was infested with the creatures. Though annoying, it didn't seem right to exterminate them. But perhaps it was time to relocate them overseas. Green Vallis, Wisconsin, was hardly suitable goblin territory, and the magick that radiated from the earth only fed the power needed for the gremians' naughty antics.

Raibeart watched the leaves swaying in the moonlight. A few shots of whiskey warmed his blood. He always took a couple before his nightly run.

The MacGregors weren't the only ones drawn to the source of power emanating from the ley lines in the area. Since his family had moved to the state, they'd had run-ins with banshees, wraiths, time-traveling curses, demons, spirits, vampires, statues, and poisonous cookies. There was also a very annoying squirrel who had dropped a nut on his nuts while he was sleeping under a tree the week before. That was no way for a man to wake up.

The rustling of the leaves brought him back to the present. The gremians came closer before suddenly stopping overhead. He grimaced, lying on his back in the dirt while waiting to see if the creatures would pass over him.

A pair of what Raibeart could only assume were brothers had insisted that he marry their sister. It figured that the one single female he *hadn't* asked to marry him had been the only one to say yes. His future would-be bride had fashioned a veil out of a torn piece of a lacy tablecloth. A marriage between a warlock and a gremian would never work for *obvious* reasons—warlocks loved for eternity, and gremians were less than monogamous.

A short series of screeches reverberated over the darkness.

"For fuck's sake, stop. I don't wish to hurt ya," Raibeart grumbled moments before gremians dropped from the trees like twisted, snarling little raindrops.

Raibeart leaped up from the ground, swinging his arms. He struck one, sending it off course. It flew several yards between two trees before smacking into a trunk.

Raibeart jumped over the log and took off in a sprint. Feet drummed behind him, the pattering sound causing him to move faster. His bare feet weren't affected by the forest floor. Warlock magick protected them well enough. Running naked wasn't exactly naked if a man had to put on boots.

The truth was, it didn't matter if he was chased. He'd still be out in the night, running himself until pure exhaustion took over. It was the only way he could fall asleep and dull the night-mares that had plagued him for hundreds of years.

He darted past the underbrush, feeling it tickle his thigh. A low branch hung over the path, and he grabbed hold to use it as leverage as he ducked beneath. The old limb cracked under his weight. Raibeart landed on his back with a thud. The rotted branch fell on his chest, and the air rushed from his lungs. "*Oof.*"

The gremians converged.

"Off, ya wee pests." Raibeart flung his arms to push them off as he tried to move out from under the branch. He could have easily used his magick, but that hardly seemed fair.

Claws dug into his inner hip a little too close to his dangly bits.

"Och!" Defensive magick erupted from him, the yellow stream instantly petrifying the critters. They froze like monstrous effigies in various positions. He gingerly pulled the stone-like claws from his hip before rolling on his side and pushing to his hands and knees. Blood trickled down his leg from the wound.

He picked up a particularly snarly creature and held it under the arms. The small mouth remained open in a now-silenced screech as saliva gripped off his chin.

"Come on then, ya wee fiend," Raibeart told the gremian. The creature couldn't hear him. He'd be in a deep sleep. "The magick will wear off, but let's put ya somewhere safe until then."

He carried it with one hand and grabbed a second creature. He found a small alcove beneath some bushes to hide them under. He made several trips back and forth. The last gremian he picked up was his would-be bride. Her lips were parted as if she were about to bite. The tablecloth veil stuck out in a permanent flutter.

"Don't ya worry, lassie," Raibeart told the gremian. "Ya will find a husband or two or three someday. I just cannot be one of them. But I'll tell ya a secret. I know my soul mate is out there. I just have to keep asking every available woman I meet. The right one will say aye."

"Hello, Da."

Raibeart nearly dropped the gremian bride. The sound of footsteps crunched the leaves. Until that moment, he hadn't heard an approach.

"Show yourself," he commanded.

Raibeart held the petrified creature and faced the path. Blue locator lights danced toward the sky like fairies in the dark forest, illuminating the location of two people. Other smaller lights came from forest animals. The moment was too brief for him to make out the details of the men's faces. Petrified, the gremians did not glow.

"Da," a second voice acknowledged.

The men weren't related to him. He would have recognized the Scottish accents if it had been a couple of his nephews trying to play a prank.

"Who are ya?" Raibeart studied them in the shadows. They were roughly the same build and age. He bounced a sphere of magick in his hand before letting it fizzle. The blue light illuminated identical faces. Twins.

"Donovan," the first answered.

"Gregory," the second said.

"Ya boys are mistaken. I think I'd remember

having sons," Raibeart dismissed. "Your chins do look a bit like that of a man I knew in Ireland. He had warts on his feet and smelled of the pasture. Is that whom ya are lookin' for?"

The men shared a look.

Raibeart gave a meaningful nod toward their feet. "Ya know, my sister Cait has a cream that will take care of warts."

"We're looking for Raibeart Donovan Gregory MacGregor," Donovan stated.

"Of the MacGregor warlocks," Gregory added.

"That's my name." He felt bad for the men. "I'm not sure what your ma told ya, laddies, but I would know if I had children. My potency is strong, but I cast a spell against repopulating the world until marriage."

"How very Victorian of ya," Donovan muttered.

"We don't have time for this nonsense," Gregory said to his brother. "She's waking up."

Raibeart studied the gremian bride and shook his head. "No need to be frightened. She won't wake for some time. I petrified her for the night."

"Put your girlfriend down." Gregory sounded exasperated. "Let's get this over with."

Raibeart set the gremian statue on the ground, if only to keep her safe before moving toward the men.

Magick stirred over his hand as he prepared for the unknown. "I must warn ya. I will defend myself."

"Ya will try," Gregory answered, not moving from the path.

"Why is he always naked?" Donovan grumbled to his twin. The brothers wore jeans and plaid flannel shirts.

Raibeart chuckled.

"If ya must ask about the choice, ya will never understand it. Ya boys' tartans are on the wrong end." Raibeart kept the magick ready, swirling it around his fingers like a snake slithering through reeds. "Now, what is it ya are after? There is no need to pretend we're related. If ya need help, the MacGregors will help ya."

"Shh." Gregory held up his hands and looked up at the treetops. "She's awake now."

Raibeart frowned, unsure what the two were going on about. He tilted his head, not hearing anything but the rustling of leaves as the breeze picked up.

Donovan ducked his head as if bracing for an attack from an unseen, unheard entity. He reached into his pocket to pull out a small pouch.

"Have ya lads been drinking? Starting to see things that aren't there?" Raibeart asked. He wasn't sure if they were a threat or needed assistance. "Ya can tell me. There's no shame in not holdin' your liquor. We've all been there. Trust me. I could tell ya stories."

Gregory plugged his ears.

"Now that's not very nice," Raibeart scolded.

"Hold this." Donovan dumped the contents of the pouch into his hand. He held a stone between two fingers to show Raibeart before tossing it at him.

Raibeart automatically caught it as his magick retreated into his body. Warmth tingled down his arm, and he could not let go of the stone as his fist clenched around it.

A high-pitched shriek erupted over the forest, shrill enough to make ears bleed. Raibeart cried out in surprise. He pressed his fists against the side of his head. He fell to his knees in the underbrush, sharp twigs from a bush scraping against his thighs. Blood streamed from his nose, running down his chest.

The shriek reverberated through his hands until he felt like his brain might explode. No thoughts circled through his mind, only the agony of the moment and the driving desire for it to end by any means.

He caught a glimpse of the twins watching him. They grimaced as if they could hear the lethal call, but it did not injure them the way it did him.

"Why?" he tried to ask, but the word came out as a scream. He fell to his side, his head buried in prickly stems.

At that moment, Raibeart understood one indisputable truth. This was all part of how a warlock died.

Chapter Three

Scotland, Winter 1558

They were at war with England.

When were they not?

Raibeart of the Clan MacGregor had fought beside his countrymen for centuries. At times, in the heat of battle, he could barely remember under which royal cause he fought. What he did know was that he'd seen too much of death.

One would think that, as warlocks, they could have won the war with magick. Unfortunately, the English had magick on their side as well, and if the MacGregors started throwing power at the opposing army, so too would the English warlocks' counterattack. Keeping magick a secret had become the one thing they could all agree on. Not even the men fighting beside him knew the truth.

Even in the stillness, the echoes of battle filled the countryside. In the dawn, when fog coated the land, he could detect the dead fighting an eternal war.

As a warlock, he could handle the cold winters of his homeland. The sweep of weather had given a short reprieve to the hostility, and he could slip away.

Slip away to her.

He walked for what felt like an eternity, and a single moment rolled into one. The rhythm of his steps crunching on the ground created a pattern of sound that lulled his senses. He couldn't remember where he'd come from or where he was going.

Crunch. Crunch. Crunch.

The landscape along his peripheral faded into a fog, blending into an impression of light pastels. Time lost meaning, as it often did in dream worlds.

The first moment he saw her, she was outside carrying a basket of vegetables. She wore a dress that had not been considered fine for nearly two decades, yet she held herself like a queen.

She was the most beautiful woman he'd ever seen. Not because other men or society would deem it so, but because when he looked at her, he felt as if all the magick, from all the ages, welled inside of him.

Crunch. Crunch.

He thought of her with her basket, of her standing on a high cliff with the wind twisting her hair, of a soft smile before he kissed her for the first time.

His steps quickened.

Crunch. Crunch. Crunch.

It had been his desire to take her away to a safe castle, to give her anything and everything. But that was not what she wanted. She didn't want to be locked away in a castle. She had brothers and uncles and a father fighting the good fight. She had a mother and sister who needed her help to maintain the land while the men were away.

Raibeart wanted to fix everything for her with magick.

He could not. That was not how the world worked.

Crunch.

His feet stopped.

When he looked up from the ground, he was not near her village as he should have been. Time felt out of sequence. He should not have been at the cliffs.

"It's too soon for this," he whispered, wanting

to back away from the moment. A feeling of dread overcame him, and he did not want to be there. He tried to shake the dream loose.

"She knows about us," a disembodied voice whispered. Her accent gave away her English birth. "She knows you betrayed her."

He began to run even before his gaze went to the distance. He found a silhouette on a cliff in the evening light. One moment it was there, the next nothing.

The voice rang out in laughter. "I told you your pet would never last."

His heart stopped beating, and in a fleeting moment of clarity, Raibeart understood the truth.

This was how a warlock died.

Chapter Four

Raibeart groaned as he held his head, wondering if he was dead.

Which nephew had magick spiked his whiskey this time? He's spent half the night convinced he was a squirrel and the other half having strange nightmares of being back in the old wars. The nightmares weren't new, but the vividness had made them feel real, and it took him a moment to reason which world was reality—battle screams or the thick bush prickling his face.

His palm throbbed as he pressed it against the forest floor. Flinching, he drew his hand into the dim light. A circle had been burned into his flesh.

He heard a soft whine while the nearby leaves rustled. Raibeart turned to see the gremian bride's hand twitch against a bush and her eyes move. She'd been petrified and had just begun to thaw.

"What happened to…?" He frowned, vaguely remembering having used his magick.

Knowing he wanted to be far away when the gremians woke up, he hopped to his feet and made his way to the nearest path. Dried blood had trailed down his thigh from his hip, but the wound had already healed. He turned in a small circle, trying to get his bearings for the walk home.

Suppressing a yawn, he waved his hand and whistled. The tartan of his kilt blurred as it flew down the path to wrap itself around his waist. He jogged in the direction the clothing had come, knowing he would have discarded his kilt early in his run. That would be the way home.

Probably.

A familiar ache inside Raibeart's chest began to grow. By the afternoon, it would feel like several bricks sitting on his heart. As the sun set, it would start to consume him. Liquor helped some…when it wasn't tainted by a magickal prank. Staying busy distracted his mind. Running himself into exhaustion each night kept the nightmares at bay.

The feeling of desperation he'd had in the bad dreams hung around him like fog over the land. He could make out the shape of reality just beyond the ethereal sky that clung sadly to it. He felt like this often, like a ghost running naked through the world, trying to anchor himself to the current reality.

Raibeart was not by nature a melancholy person. In fact, he was quite the opposite, but that did not mean that part of him didn't exist. If he let himself wallow, he could feel lonely in a crowded room. Instead, he chose to focus on things outside of himself, like his family.

Family.

His nephews and nieces had been given a lucky run of things. They'd been finding love left and right. Partners seemed to be dropping out of the sky into their laps after hundreds of years of searching. Even his brother, Fergus, had found the resurrected spirit of his lost love.

Raibeart didn't want to take all the credit, but he was pretty sure some of the spells he'd been using to draw love to himself had affected the other MacGregors instead. His family believed it was due to the magickal ley lines under the town where they now lived. The current created an invisible river underground where centuries of residual magick bound together. People always assumed magick just appeared out of (and dissipated into) nothing. That wasn't true. Magick needed energy to manifest. Warlocks pulled life from nature to fuel their powers. That's why they lived near the forest, so they could take a little from each plant and leave the landscape unscathed.

Fantastic sex would also build up energy for a nice surge. Raibeart missed sex. Ever since he'd had a run-in with an inthrall, sex usually left him feeling hollow.

It was like a curse kept him from finding his *fiorghrá*, his true love. Not that he intended to stop trying. He asked every woman he met to marry him. Eventually, the right one would say yes. A crone he'd bought drinks at an English tavern once told him love was a numbers game and he needed to try harder. Her words had made sense. Fate had a lot to do, and he didn't want to miss his chance.

The MacGregor property totaled about eighty acres of beautiful nature—a forest with hiking paths, a small stream, and manicured house gardens. It was enough to fuel the entire family's magick. Raibeart felt the expanse of trees stretching out around him, the subtle energy ready to be siphoned should he need it.

The fresh air filled his lungs and steadied his thoughts. He preferred this Wisconsin home over New York City. Living near Central Park had left him feeling closed in, the rectangular boundaries and dense population making it hard to enjoy his nightly runs. Reports of the Central Park Streaker had been a point of contention with his family— even though Raibeart had been innocent.

The MacGregor mansion graced the top of a hill overlooking the town below. There were several outbuildings, including a converted garage from an 1800s coach house. Raibeart liked knowing his family was close and preferred it when they all lived in the same home. Perhaps he was old-fashioned, stuck in the days when High- lander clans were bound together by necessity and love. Though Wisconsin was no Scotland, and part of his spirit would always remain in his homeland.

The Georgian-style house had over sixty-five rooms with enough bedrooms to fit his nieces and nephews, their spouses, and his three brothers and their wives. Sadly, many of the younger genera- tion had moved out, opting to live with their spouses in other parts of town. He supposed that their living inside city limits was close enough. Raibeart made a point of night-running near each of them as often as possible to check that they were safe.

Raibeart looked down the long drive. It was the only way to and from the house that didn't include a trek through the wilderness. A few streetlights still shone as last holdouts to the dawn.

Coming up the house's front steps, he waved his hand to magickly open the door as he strode inside. The sound of laughter came from the dining room. He paused, taking a deep breath, and smiling at hearing his extended family.

"When we first came here, they didn't have buried cable for phone and internet." His nephew Euann's voice carried from the other room.

Euann loved technology, a strange yet harmless hobby. Raibeart used to think computers and smartphones were ridiculous until he discovered social media. A lot of single ladies used the internet. He particularly liked romance book clubs. Those women were romantically inclined and couldn't resist the videos he posted dancing in a kilt. Plus posting marriage proposals online was a great way to cover broader territory.

"Remember that storm Erik caused when he went screwy after we first moved here?" Euann continued. "All the old phone lines blew down? People were…ya know what? Never mind. If it were left to ya Neanderthals, we'd still be in the Middle Ages enchanting carrier pigeons."

"Do ya still have the footage of Erik singing to Lydia on her front lawn when he was under that love potion spell?" Iain asked. He was Euann's brother, another of Raibeart's many nephews. "I think it's time for that video to resurface. I want to buy ad space for it at the movie theater to play before the shows."

"I'd forgotten about those pigeons," Angus said, bringing the subject back around. "Margareta, what was that bird's name? The one Raibeart enchanted to fly dirty limericks across enemy lines?"

"Oh, that's right!" Margareta laughed. "The messages were brought to the commander and not his mistress."

"Innis," Raibeart answered as he joined them. Euann and Iain sat at the table with their parents, Angus and Margareta. They stared at him like he'd sprouted a second head. He heard the sound of banging pans coming from the kitchen. "The name of the bird, not the mistress."

"Right, Innis." Angus nodded. His long beard had been recently trimmed. Margareta had been threatening to cut it off.

"What happened?" Margareta demanded, pushing up from her chair.

Hundreds of years could not diminish his sister-by-marriage's beauty or her determined gaze. Long hair was pulled back into one of those girly braided crowns like Margareta had dubbed herself Queen of the MacGregors. Her low tone gave away her concern. The calmer she was, the more exasperated she was likely to be. It was no surprise that she often sounded calm around him.

"The commander fell in love with me," Raibeart stated the obvious. "I'm irresistible."

"Cait!" Margareta called. "You're needed."

Cait appeared in the doorway. She had married his brother Murdoch centuries ago. She liked to dress like a prim and proper lady, but he'd seen her drunk on the moors howling at the moon after a fistfight. Her rigid demeanor seemed to war with Margareta's determination in their need to be the matriarch of the family, though they shared that honor.

"What happened to your face?" Cait asked.

"It's always been this handsome," Raibeart said. He smelled something cooking. "What are ya making? Danish?"

"Quiche," Cait said.

Raibeart grimaced. "Poor use of an egg. I think it would much rather be made into a Danish."

"Were you attacked?" Margareta asked. "Where did the blood come from?"

Raibeart crossed to a window to catch his reflection. Dried blood trailed from his nose and ears. "Huh, look at that. Must have been a couple of gremians."

He gave a dismissive wave of his hand.

"Gremians don't cause that kind of damage," Cait stated. "Raibeart, sit down. Angus, get a wet washcloth."

Angus went to the kitchen. Raibeart obeyed Cait's command. He'd lived long enough to know that there was no use fighting the women in the family when they set their minds to fussing over something. Seeing a mug in front of Iain, Raibeart held out his hand and magickly slid it toward him. He caught it against his palm.

"Hey!" Iain protested.

Raibeart took a drink and frowned at the offensive flavor. "Tastes funny."

"It's coffee," Iain answered.

"Tastes like a candy cane buggered a sugar cookie and shat out—" Raibeart began.

"Language!" Cait scolded.

Raibeart cocked a half smile and repeated the entire sentiment in Gaelic.

Cait sighed and shook her head. She snapped her fingers to produce a glow and pulled at his earlobe to look inside. "I don't see any damage."

"Look again," Iain snickered, prompting Euann to do the same. "I'm sure it's in there."

Raibeart waved his hand to send the offensive coffee flying toward its rightful owner. Iain half-cried out, half-laughed as he shot up from his seat.

Cait tugged at his ear. "Hold still."

"Ow!" Raibeart lightly swatted at her hand. "It's fine. Though I could have ya look at this."

He held out his palm for her inspection. Cait automatically went to work examining the burn, pressing the surrounding skin.

"If ya feel friction, you're holding it too tight," Iain drawled.

Margareta shot her son a correcting look at the crude joke.

"Margareta, love, would ya fetch me a coffee with a splash of the hot stuff?" Raibeart asked.

"No," Margareta answered, "but I'll get ya a coffee with creamer."

"What is...?" Cait sniffed his hand. "There's something familiar about this. I sense a magick residue."

"Woke up with it," Raibeart said.

"I'll get a salve." Cait dropped his hand and left the dining room.

Angus crossed paths with her in the doorway. He tossed a wet washcloth at Raibeart's head.

Raibeart didn't bother trying to catch it as it landed over his face. He peered through the tiny holes in the terrycloth, seeing blurry bits of light coming through. It brought to mind an image from long ago of light coming through a bolt of material as a delicate hand inspected it.

The image sent a jolt of panic through him,

and he ripped the cloth off his face and threw it like it was on fire. His chair fell back as he stumbled away from it.

His family stared at him, not reacting otherwise.

"What was that?" Raibeart demanded. His heart beat a little too fast, and he felt sick with worry.

"A washcloth," Angus answered dryly.

"Something isn't right with this reality." Raibeart waved his hand to encompass the dining room. He watched the colors on the wall fade from blue to green to off-white. The styles of the chairs altered, the backs growing taller. No one else appeared to notice the subtle changes.

Iain stood. A jacket magickly appeared over his t-shirt though his kilt remained the same. "Jane is expecting a shipment of fertilizer and pots today. I promised to help her unload."

Euann disappeared mid-drink to be replaced by his brother, Erik.

"Business going well for her?" Angus's beard vanished to show a clean-shaven face.

Erik set the cup down on the table.

"Mrs. Callister's blog posts insinuating we are secret pot farmers actually helped business." Iain chuckled. "Jane thinks we should send her a thank ya card. Which reminds me, we want to talk to the family about putting an extra greenhouse north of the garage."

"I'll put it up for a vote at the next meeting." Angus's beard reappeared, longer and scragglier than before.

"Where's Jewel?" Raibeart went to look in the foyer for her. As a phoenix, the child had unlimited power. If the young girl were playing, that would explain why the environment was changing, and no one else seemed to notice. Raibeart felt a kinship with the girl. Until recently, she'd kept dying and being reborn. The poor thing had yet to make it to her teen years. They were hopeful that this incarnation would survive.

"Andrea and Kenneth took her to New Orleans to stay with Andrea's grandmama Ruth and aunt Florence. They're teaching her their kind of magick," Margareta said. Jewel was her only grandchild, and she fretted endlessly over the girl. "Ya know this. Ya helped them pack."

Raibeart didn't remember doing any such thing. He shook his head to indicate as much.

"Ya insisted on sending seven pairs of fairy wings and those awful plastic and sequined shoes ya let her pick out in the toy catalog and made Malina materialize," Margareta continued.

Raibeart again shook his head. He'd just gotten out of a repeating time loop with his niece

Maura and her dhampir husband. It took forever to break the old vampire's curse, and Raibeart had been the only one aware of what was happening at the time. He wasn't about to leap happily into another quest.

"We all discussed this. I know ya love playing with her, but that child has been tapping into too much magick. We can't keep expecting a child to bail us out of supernatural trouble. She can't be around here right now. Kenneth is afraid she's going to flame out again and be reborn. We just want her to reach adulthood." Margareta sighed. "Are ya having another one of your episodes?"

"There's a curse," Raibeart said, knowing from experience that everyone was going to dismiss his warning. "Something's not right."

"Go wash the night off," Margareta responded with a little prod toward the direction of his bedroom. When he glanced at her, her hair was cut short. "Start the day right."

Raibeart sighed. He wasn't sure why he could sense things others couldn't. Being the most intelligent person in the room could be a burden. Sometimes he wished he could be ignorant.

"Is he acting stranger than usual?" Euann was asking when Raibeart returned. He'd replaced Erik and sat in his original spot.

Cait tossed a small jar at him. "Keep that on it."

"Uncle Raibeart, ya want to help me at the greenhouse today?" Iain asked. "We would appreciate it. Jane hates it when we use her plants to fuel our magick, so it'll be all manual labor."

"Nice try, laddie." Raibeart wasn't about to volunteer for fertilizer duty. "I have to make the rounds. I hear a new ER nurse is starting at the hospital today. I'm going to take her temperature and see if she wants a husband."

"Aren't they supposed to take *your*...?" Euann waved his hand to dismiss the rest of the thought. "Good luck. Try not to get arrested."

"Crimson Tavern tonight," Raibeart stated by way of an invitation to anyone who cared to join him.

He went through the kitchen before going down the long hall toward his room. His nieces and nephews lived on the top floor of the home. The elders had taken the wing past the kitchen. There they kept their bedroom suites and offices.

The MacGregor Empire had grown an almost ridiculous amount as the years went by. They had their hand in biotech, charities, hotels, restaurants, manufacturing plants, and countless small businesses. It seemed they were determined to acquire, always adding. Sometimes he missed the freedom of no responsibility.

But if he had to decide which business to get out of, he couldn't do it. Too many people depended on them. Whenever they moved to a new location, they ensured the area thrived. They created jobs and protected the people under their care—not that the locals knew they needed protection.

Raibeart's bedroom looked exactly like it had for hundreds of years. Magick placed each stone along the wall and floor and lit the fireplace. He felt no reason to change it. There was a comfort to the familiar. Even though he didn't sleep in the large bed, he kept it like a shrine to something he'd forgotten long ago. He wasn't sure what the thing was, exactly, that he should remember, but it was a feeling. Dark steps led up to the mattress like it was a stage, and wooden posts flanked the corners.

His portrait hung over the mantel. That was one thing that did not come from the Middle Ages. Everyone in the family had one painted. Most stood in the Highlands with kilts blowing in the air. Raibeart had posed nude using his old kilt as a blanket, fully splayed and erect, with a rose in his mouth.

He frowned as the rose changed from white to yellow.

"Who's doing that?" he asked the empty room.

His comforter turned from crimson and gold to green. He felt as if someone had turned his heart upside-down in daring to touch the memory shrine.

"That goes too far," Raibeart shouted. "Show yourself."

He waited for the blue lights to reveal someone. No one appeared.

Raibeart's bathroom looked nothing like his bedroom, with its flat white tiles and shiny porcelain. He paused at the door and then decided to skip the shower. He waved his hand over his face and head, using magick to clean himself. The family tried not to overuse their powers, but he was in no mood to do things the human way.

When he turned back around, his bed had been changed to mattresses hanging low from the ceiling by chains.

"Oh, that's gone too far. Ya don't touch a man's love nest," Raibeart declared. He marched out of the room and cried, "Batten down the hatches and lock the doors, laddies. Bad magick is afoot, and she stole my bed!"

Chapter Five

Katherine's eyes opened to the familiar cottage ceiling. Sometimes she wished she could just stay asleep forever. Dreamless nights were the best. She used to think dreams were a salvation, as they connected her to feelings she'd lost, but with time those became a torment.

"My name is Katherine Galbraith," she whispered, partly to remind herself who she was, and partly to hear the sound of her own voice, so she remembered how to speak. "This is not my home. I am a prisoner of magick for loving a warlock. I had a father, a mother, and three brothers. They died. My name is Katherine, and I cannot die."

No voice answered back.

She pushed up from the bed in her usual routine, automatically taking the covers with her.

She dragged the blanket out of the room and down the hall. Averting her gaze, she draped the material over the mirror so she wouldn't accidentally see the world beyond.

Each step was one she'd walked a million times, like a ghost roaming empty halls, locked in her small world.

Was this the afterlife?

Was this Hell?

"I am a prisoner of magick," she whispered as a mantra so as not to forget. Unfortunately, the simple statement didn't give her any details about how, who, or why.

She hurried toward the cracked wall where she'd stood staring until she fainted, only to awake back in bed. Her eyes scanned the plaster, desperate to find the abnormality. She ran her hands along the wall, searching where the crack had been.

Nothing.

The anomaly was gone, completely repaired as if it had never existed.

"No," she cried softly, hitting the wall with her fist so hard that it bruised a knuckle. She fell to her knees. Her hand throbbed.

Katherine trembled as she choked on her tears. She slapped the wall with her uninjured hand as hard as she could, then again and again, until finally she tore across the room to grab a dining chair.

"Let me out," she pleaded. "Please, just let me go."

She screamed as she smashed the furniture against the wall. A piece splintered, cutting her hand.

No one answered.

What had she done to deserve this? Surely there was something long ago and forgotten. Something horrible and depraved. Why else would she be here?

"I am a prisoner of magick for loving a warlock."

Katherine stood. Those words didn't really answer the questions. Had they ever made sense? Was the warlock evil? Did he trick her? Had she tricked him?

The raw wound throbbed as she rushed back to the bedroom, dripping blood quietly on the floor. The house always righted itself, and the broken chair would not be there later.

She brushed past the mirror and heard the covers drop onto the floor. She saw movement within the glass that did not match her passing reflection. She refused the temptation to look.

Inside the bedchamber, above the fireplace, hung a painting of a handsome warlock in front of a castle. Next to him, a lady clung possessively to his arm. Her dark hair and eyes radiated beauty, as did her elegant gown. The noblewoman smiled, the slight half-curl of her lips sending a chill through Katherine each time she looked at the couple.

Had he been married? Was that a wife?

"What did I do?"

To her shame, Katherine felt a remnant of feelings for the man. Maybe it was more of an echo that she clung to because she had nothing else.

"No man is worth this," she told the painting. "I can't remember what I loved about ya."

Sadly, it was the truth. All the love she'd felt had faded over time along with her memory. All that was left was a cold emptiness as she faced eternal banishment.

A light flutter sounded behind her, and she looked to see what happened. The bedcovers had returned, only this time they were green, not red. A slight scraping noise had her rotating back to the painting. The woman had disappeared, and the warlock lay naked on a kilt. The sexual image took her by surprise. He held a vaguely familiar flower in his mouth.

The bedroom door slammed shut, and she jumped in alarm. Her breath caught, and she had to force herself to exhale. Air came out in shaky pants.

Anticipation more than fear filled her. The stone beneath her feet shifted, moving as it changed configurations. She glanced over the room before watching the door. The handle transformed, becoming round. She twirled in a circle and searched for other variations.

"Let this be over."

Katherine wanted it all to end. She wanted the cottage to crumble over her, burying her under the heavy stones and beams.

"Let this be—"

"It was red and now it's green." A strong male voice cut off her whisper.

Katherine stared at the door. She watched the knob turn. It sounded strange to hear a voice that was not her own.

"Raibeart, why don't ya come back into the dining room and sit down," someone soothed. "Who would want to steal your bed?"

Katherine held still, listening to the conversation.

"Ya never believe me, Cait, but I am rarely wrong," the man insisted. "When Maura was stuck in the time loop, I told ya so. I was right. No one listened. I had to watch them go round and round and round and—"

"I get your point," Cait interjected.

"—round while the rest of the world stopped," Raibeart said.

"I don't remember ya saying anything about that," Cait denied.

"Of course, ya don't. I didn't tell ya in the last loop when the curse was broken," Raibeart answered.

"Fine, show me this magickal bedspread threat," Cait said.

The door opened.

Katherine held still, watching to see what would happen. No part of her thought to hide.

The warlock from the painting entered and froze in surprise to see her. He looked a little older, but not by much. His long brown hair hung wild with a small twig sticking from within. His kilt appeared the same, if not a little disheveled, and he wore no shirt or boots.

A strange mix of feelings stirred inside Katherine. She wanted to run. She wanted to attack. She wanted to scream.

She didn't move.

The woman entered behind him, nudging him out of her way. Raibeart shuffled aside but otherwise kept the same position.

Cait stopped short when she saw Katherine and planted her hand on her hips. She wore a skirt that only went to her knees and a flowing shirt without a corset to tame its shape. Katherine had seen such styles in the mirror.

"Is this your decorating demon? She hardly looks threatening." Cait gave a small laugh. "Where did ya find her? The Renaissance Faire?"

Cait did not look like the woman in the portrait who'd stared at her all those nights.

"I'm Cait MacGregor," she said. "I am married to Raibeart's brother."

"Who are ya?" Raibeart's tone had softened from when he'd talked to his sister-by-marriage. "How did ya come to be in my bedroom?"

He looked at her expectantly. No. He stared at her.

"Miss?" Cait insisted, her expression falling some with concern.

It had been a long time since someone had spoken to her, and it took Katherine a moment to respond. She looked back and forth between the two.

"M-my name is Katherine Galbraith," she whispered, unsure of what else to say. "This is not my home." She took a deep breath, and her words continued, slow and shaky. "I am a prisoner of magick for loving a warlock. I had a father, a mother, and three brothers. They died. My name is Katherine, and I cannot die."

"She's in shock." Cait looked at Raibeart. "Where did ya find her?"

Raibeart pointed toward the floor. "Right there, just now."

Cait approached slowly. "Katherine, how did ya get here? What happened to ya? Who hurt your family?"

"My name is Katherine," she whispered, unable to answer the woman's questions. "I cannot die."

Chapter Six

"I cannot die."

Raibeart's magick surged, siphoning fuel through his bedroom window from the outside forest as it readied for a fight. He didn't know what was happening, but he felt he had to protect this woman at all costs. Confusion filled her eyes outdone only by her fear. He found himself staring into them, sucked into an abyss of emotion, unable to pull away.

The sounds of a battle echoed through his thoughts, not guns and explosions but the old clank of swords and groaning wood.

A warning? A memory? A dream?

He touched his hand to feel that he wasn't in a dream, and this was happening.

"My name is Katherine," she whispered again,

as if not knowing what else to say. She searched his face, expecting the name to mean something to him. "Katherine."

For the first time in a long time, Raibeart felt his mind become clearer, and the thoughts stopped rushing around in his brain.

There was something familiar about the woman as if he'd once touched the soft curve of her hip hidden by the long dressing gown she wore. Ladies didn't wear that style of nightclothes anymore. Dark auburn hair caught the light coming from the fireplace. Brown eyes watched him warily as if she knew him but feared him.

Why would she fear him?

"My name is Katherine," the woman insisted.

"All right, Katherine, all right," Cait answered. "You're safe now. Tell us what happened. Did warlock magick do this?"

Katherine glanced back and forth between them and then slowly nodded.

"Can ya tell me which warlock hurt ya?" Cait persisted.

Katherine stared at Raibeart. They waited, but she declined to answer.

Cait didn't let up. "We can't help ya if ya don't let us."

"I am a prisoner of magick," Katherine said.

Raibeart wanted to find the person who had

wronged her. Everything inside of him told him to hold her and not let go. He would find who had hurt her and he would protect her.

"Whose prisoner?" Cait asked.

"I…" Katherine shook her head.

The urge to reach for her grew stronger. Raibeart wanted to touch her and make sure she was real. He felt magick all around them as if it created a wall between him and the woman.

Katherine turned to glance up at his portrait over the fireplace. He followed her gaze. Instead of the nude, another picture of him took its place.

Raibeart frowned. He stood in front of a castle, looking boring and regal. Next to him was a woman he didn't recognize.

"Raibeart?" Cait also looked at the portrait. "I don't remember…"

"I told ya. Everything is changing," he said, relieved that for once, someone else appeared to notice the difference.

"Who is that woman?" Cait asked. "Why is she in your portrait? Is this some sort of prank?"

Raibeart frowned. "I don't know her."

"She's not your wife?" Katherine asked.

Raibeart shook his head. "I'm not married."

"Betrothed?" Katherine asked.

Cait suppressed a laugh.

"It's not from a lack of trying if ya know what

I mean." Raibeart winked, trying to lighten the mood. It didn't work.

Katherine's brow furrowed.

Cait waved for him to move aside.

"Let's get ya some hot tea, Katherine," Cait soothed, reaching to touch Katherine's arm.

Katherine jerked away from the contact and rubbed at the spot like she could erase the sensation. "How did ya get in here? No one has ever come in here."

"Ya are in our home," Raibeart said. "This is my room. I come in here daily."

Katherine shook her head in denial, not believing him. She took a hesitant step toward him. Raibeart offered his hand to her. She eyed it as she moved around him, careful not to touch him as she stayed out of reach. She went into the hallway.

"This isn't right." Katherine looked around. "This shouldn't be here."

Raibeart and Cait followed her into the hall. She backed away from them, glancing over her shoulder to see the path. Her fingers trailed over the hallway wall as if to guide her.

Raibeart's instinct was to hurry after her. Cait put a hand on his arm to slow his steps.

"Don't force her to take our help," Cait said. "She knows we offered."

Katherine's fingers hit a doorframe, and she jerked her hand back. She turned in a panic, running away from them.

"Wait, lassie." Raibeart went after her. "We'll not hurt ya."

She pushed open a couple of the bedroom doors before continuing to flee toward the kitchen.

"Cait, my love?" Murdoch called from the kitchen, looking for his wife. He appeared in front of Katherine. "Oh, a visitor. Hello, lady, welcome to—"

Katherine changed course before reaching Murdoch. She darted to the left, bursting out the back door into the gardens.

"Raibeart, who was that woman?" Cait demanded, her tone not as soft as before. "She did not look as if she wanted to be here. And what was that about her family dying?"

"I have never seen her." Raibeart went after Katherine to offer help.

"Ask another one to marry him, did he? Looks like she's a runner," Murdoch said to his wife with a chuckle. "Please tell me he's not keeping potential brides locked up in his room now."

"If he is, we're going to have to seriously discuss having him committed," Cait answered.

Raibeart ignored them.

The back walking gardens technically

consisted of six acres. Manicured bushes and paths created an oasis and reminded him of the old English palace gardens. Trees from the forest had overtaken a large section, and it wasn't unusual to run into fountains and statues within the trees.

"Show yourself," he whispered, watching for the twinkly blue lights to guide him to Katherine. She'd taken one of the paths into the forest.

Daylight filtered through the trees, creating easy travel. He heard her footsteps and listened to their stuttering as she stopped and started. His only goal was to keep watch. Something pulled him after her but also told him to keep his distance. Like before, he sensed an invisible wall between them, a flow of air that would refuse to let him pass over to her side.

Magick surged through his body, having escalated the first moment he looked at her. Now it hummed in his veins and tingled the tips of his fingers.

If he were honest, his fingers weren't the only tips that tingled. Beneath his kilt, his cock began to twitch in excitement. The Happy Scotsman wanted to make an appearance.

"Down, laddie," Raibeart instructed himself.

That part of his body did not listen to commands.

To be fair, the other parts of him weren't too keen on taking orders either.

Katherine stood in the path facing him. Raibeart had been so preoccupied with his arousal that he'd not realized she'd stopped and waited. Her mouth opened, but she struggled to speak.

The magick continued to churn inside him and suddenly leaked out, swirling through the air to dance around her. She gasped, swatting her arms as if she could get it away from her. The magick settled on her skin, and she inhaled deeply. Her wild eyes cleared by small degrees, and she again turned her attention to him.

"What is this new game?" Her words sounded more confident as if his magick had calmed her and given her the words she'd been missing before. "None of this is as it should be."

Though it had been unintentional, Raibeart was glad that his magick helped her. Even when he didn't know the right thing to do, his magick often did. Magick was simply a shifting of energy from plants to him to some form of power. It saw the void inside of her and filled it with what she needed. So many in his family felt the need to practice and control their abilities. Not Raibeart. He gave himself over to them entirely. Maybe that was why he saw things others couldn't.

"I love games. I'd be happy to play with ya,"

he said. Whatever she wanted, he would do. The poor lassie looked like she could use some fun in her life.

"How long until we reach the edge?" She pointed down the path.

"Edge?"

"Of the world. How far?" she insisted.

"Oh, ya are a flat earther. Sorry, lassie, but I have seen the world, and it is round." Raibeart tried to be sympathetic. "When ya sail into the horizon, ya will not fall off the side though there are sea monsters. The old maps got that much right, so be careful."

"Round? That is why I walk in loops?" She glanced behind her on the path. "How many people are here?"

"In the forest?" This was by far the strangest conversation, but Raibeart didn't mind. Most of his conversations were peculiar.

"In this world. In this prison."

"Oh, ah, not quite eight billion according to my friend the internet," he said. "Half that are women. I wanted to know my odds of finding love."

Katherine appeared confused. "Billion?"

"I haven't personally calculated them all, but apparently, someone has. Can't say I'd care for that job. Most in that total are humans, but I'm sure that includes warlocks, witches, some vampires, and shifters. I don't think they counted trolls and goblins, or fairies, gremians, sprites, spriggans, banshees, leprechauns, the animal-human hybrids, and their opposites, the human-animal hybrids, or…" Raibeart slowly nodded. "Ya make a fair point. We should do a supernatural census to check the populations. I haven't seen a minotaur in a wee while."

"I don't know what you're saying." Katherine's expression didn't lighten. "Did ya lose your love and are trying to find her?"

"Never had her." Though the truth hurt, Raibeart was never one to lie. Keeping the truth organized in his head was difficult enough.

"Then…we…weren't…? You're not…?" She shook her head. "Can I die here?"

Raibeart hated the pain he saw reflected in her eyes. She reminded him of a wild animal being hunted without understanding why someone wanted her dead. He didn't answer her because he didn't like the truth. Yes, she could die. They all could, technically. For some reason, he found it best not to tell her.

She kept her distance. Her eyes darted to the trees. More to the forest than to him, she called, "If this is a new torment, please stop. I don't want to go back to the cottage."

"We don't have to go to the cottage," Raibeart assured her. "What happened at the cottage?"

"All I know is I am a prisoner of magick for loving a warlock, but I don't love him anymore. I thought he was in the painting, but I must have remembered wrong because ya don't know who I am." She again looked at the trees. "I don't understand any of this."

Raibeart's magick remained on high alert as if trying to warn him. He didn't sense anyone in the forest, but perhaps it was best to get her out of there. Another little surge of his magick burst out of him and made its way over to her. She waved her hand in front of her face and closed her eyes as if swatting back a pest.

"Come back inside. I'm hardly one to judge running around the forest in your nightgown, but the ladies of the manor will have my head if I don't at least offer ya breakfast first. Just don't eat anything Cait offers to cook for ya. She's a talented healer, but her food isn't fit for a troll prison."

Katherine looked down at her clothes. "They didn't change."

"From what?"

"In the morning, when I walk out of the bedchambers, my nightclothes usually transform into the same gown." She came a little closer, taking small steps in his direction.

"I have an enchanted kilt," Raibeart said by way of conversation. He, too, took another step to close the distance between them. "It finds me every morning."

"Just the kilt, though." She nodded at his naked chest.

"Aye." He smiled. To his pleasure, he saw the corner of her mouth lift ever so slightly. The mood lightened but the invisible barrier between them remained. "For some reason, humans frown upon a man enjoying the full freedom of nature. If they catch me naked, they try to put me in the drunk tank."

"I know what a drunk tank is. How do I know what that is?" She stopped within arm's reach.

His magick radiated off his chest, encompassing them within a sparkly cocoon.

"I've seen this world in a mirror. I didn't understand all its contraptions." She gazed up into his eyes. "How carriages moved without horses. How lights didn't need fire. How stairs moved when the people did not. I thought it had to be a world of magick, but it's not. It's people making things that should not be possible."

Raibeart realized what his magick was doing for her. It helped clear her mind and made sense of the world around her as if his knowledge flowed into her.

"And yet, they still do horrible things to each other," she continued. "The drunk tanks in the jails are full of unkindness, and the cells beyond those are much worse. How can the world have so many pretty things and yet be broken? Don't people know what they have?"

"Ya were in a prison?"

She nodded. "Of the worst kind. I was left alone for what must have been hundreds of years living in the same cottage. The weather sometimes changed, but nothing else. I lost count."

"Who put ya in this solitary confinement?"

"Magick, but I don't know whose. All I remember is what I've whispered to myself every morning since it happened." She closed her eyes and repeated what she'd said before. "My name is Katherine Galbraith. This is not my home. I am a prisoner of magick for loving a warlock. I had a father, a mother, and three brothers. They died. My name is Katherine, and I cannot die."

Katherine opened her eyes and took a deep breath.

"That's all I remember," she said. "I can't be sure that I didn't tell myself a lie. Maybe I did do something horrible, something I was desperate to forget. So, each morning, I lied to myself until only the lies remained. Or maybe it was true. Maybe I was wronged. Maybe it was a mistake. Maybe the warlock was married. I wish I knew the truth."

Raibeart wanted to touch her, but that invisible current was still between them. When he lifted his hand, physical pain shot up his arm to keep him away.

When she again looked at him, her gaze pleaded for help. A tear slid down her cheek. "I mean, I would have to be horrible to have deserved to be locked away by myself in a world that did not end. To see my family die in a cursed mirror without being able to help or say goodbye. To watch them search for me and assume I had died. But I was there. I was there, watching them in a mirror, screaming for them to see me. I pleaded for someone to come, anyone. I begged that mirror to let me out. I thought if I could escape, it would all make sense. But here I am. I'm out. And nothing has become clear. I still feel like I'm trapped."

Raibeart didn't try to solve her problem. It was clear she needed someone to listen, and he would be that ear for her. His magick coated them again, coaxing her to speak.

"I made myself remember every morning, but their faces have faded. I didn't have a painting for them, only the strangers staring down at me like I had broken into their house. The mirror showed me them after, but their bodies withered, and I could no longer look at the decay. When I did peek, decades later, they were bones. I feel like their voices are right on the edge of my mind, but I can't make them loud enough to hear." She moved as if to reach for him, but that same invisible current held her away. "Ya and that woman's painting hung over the fireplace. Why? Who is she?"

Raibeart waited to ensure she was done talking before saying, "I have lived for centuries. I cannot tell ya why someone would want to paint my face except that I'm told it's quite handsome."

She tilted her head and studied him. "Are ya mocking me?"

"Never."

Katherine frowned. "I don't trust ya. I can't."

"Sweet bonnie lassie, ya have had a rough go of it, haven't ya? I would never mock ya," he whispered, wanting to break through their barrier. "I know exactly what ya need. Follow me."

She didn't immediately move to go with him.

"All I can give ya is my word. I promise to do whatever I can to help ya figure this out," he said. "Please, trust me, until I give ya a reason not to."

Chapter Seven

Katherine kept her head down as they made their way around the side of a large manor. Evenly spaced windows gave her peeks inside people-less rooms. A few times, she stopped to stare inside. She knew the names of things—couch, office, books, light switch, coffee mug, desk—but it made no logical sense that she did. These were not items she had seen before.

Being near Raibeart created a combination of calm and panic inside of her. Calm because his face was so familiar. It was the only familiar thing in this strange place. Panic because, for centuries, she'd associated her prison with him.

How could she know his role in it if she couldn't remember the past? Or hers?

They stopped near the front corner of the

home. Raibeart peeked around to the front before waving for her to follow him.

"Why aren't we going inside?" she asked.

"I don't think a dose of my family is what ya need right now. They'll be full of questions and coffee and magick spells and jokes that are not as funny as they think they are." Raibeart quickly led the way to another building. "What ya need is an escape, not an inquisition."

Katherine hurried after him. What other option did she have?

He held open a door, and she rushed past him. At his nearness, she felt tiny shocks of pain work their way over her arm. Inside the building, several of the horseless carriages rested. She hesitated before touching the blue metal in the dim light, half expecting it to move. In the mirror they had made loud noises, like angry children growling at the roads. The cold of its body seeped into her fingers. She leaned her ear closer.

"First, we need..." Raibeart glanced around the garage and then pointed toward her. "These."

Clothing materialized next to her.

Raibeart turned his back.

She picked up a pair of pants. "Is an Englishman joining us?"

Raibeart glanced over his shoulder and chuckled. "Many women prefer to wear those."

"Oh. Um?" She examined the waistband, unconvinced. "I do want to look like I belong."

"Perhaps these instead?" Raibeart again pointed.

The pants disappeared from her hands to be replaced by a long skirt. That and the flowing shirt on the car were not what she was used to. Then again, she was only used to either the one set of night clothes or the one gown she'd worn for the last eternity.

"No?" Raibeart hummed softly before pointing a third time. "This."

The skirt disappeared from her hand. An earasaid appeared on top of the car. She picked up the plaid material. It matched his tartan kilt.

"I remember these," she said, running her hands over the material.

Katherine nodded at him. He turned to give her privacy.

She had taken her clothes on and off, so she remembered how to dress, even though it had not been necessary to do so in her prison. She struggled to pleat the long swath of material in preparation to wrap it around her waist. Suddenly, the fabric moved on its own, fluttering around her. The nightgown began to melt, dripping off her body like liquid as it trailed to the floor.

Katherine tried to hold on to it, but it ran over

her fingers. A white shirt flew at her, wrapping itself over her chest and arms. The material moved as if held by invisible servants. She automatically lifted her arms as the plaid circled her to create the traditional Highland dress. A belt cinched the pleated skirt into place, and the remaining length flung over her shoulder.

"I…" She faced Raibeart. He now wore a shirt and boots along with the kilt.

Raibeart grinned at her. "You're a right bonnie princess."

"It feels strange to have something new." She ran her hands along the material before smelling the fabric. She closed her eyes trying to grab onto the memory that it stirred. "I remember that smell. I went with my ma to someplace, and they had colorful bolts of material still smelling of dye. It had been so beautiful. I remember wishing I could take them all home just to release them into the air to watch them drift around me in the breeze."

When she opened her eyes, she was surrounded by strips of gauzy material hanging from the ceiling. A bright light came from behind as the wall shifted upward. The breeze caused the gauze to flutter. She gasped in pleasure and reached to touch them. The cool fabric moved with her fingers as she turned, watching the ripples she created.

"How did ya…?" She pushed the material aside to find Raibeart watching.

"Magick." He smiled.

The material fell from the ceiling to pool around her feet before disappearing.

"We should go. They would have heard the garage door." Raibeart opened a car door for her.

Katherine found a pair of short boots on the ground and pulled them on.

He motioned for her to get into the car. She examined the interior before crawling inside. She jumped in alarm when he closed the door with a heavy thud, not liking the enclosed space. She pressed her face against the glass to watch him walk around to the other side.

Raibeart entered the car and slid into the seat next to her. He had picked up her nightclothes and now pushed them into the seat behind them.

The car grunted to life, and she grabbed hold of the seat as it began to move. The world blurred around her, and she pressed her lips tightly together to hold back the nausea as they reversed. She watched a man in a kilt come out of the house, arms waving as if to get their attention.

"Sorry, Euann." Raibeart chuckled to himself.

The car jerked to a stop before changing directions, taking them down the hill.

Katherine kept her face pressed against the glass, watching the landscape as Raibeart drove. The world traveled too fast outside the window. She shifted uncomfortably in her seat.

"I do not enjoy this horseless carriage," she managed through clenched teeth.

"Try looking forward," he said.

She did. The blurring wasn't as pronounced, but it did little to calm her nerves. "These carriages go too fast."

"This is only twenty miles per hour. They go much faster." Raibeart chuckled, and the car slowed. "Is this better?"

She nodded, even though she still didn't enjoy it.

Raibeart's hands moved over the wheel, directing the metal beast. They met other cars on the road. A couple of them let loose a horrible noise and zoomed around them.

Katherine pulled her feet up onto the seat and hugged her knees. She should not have gotten inside the car with him. He had said he knew what she needed. This ride was not it.

Tall buildings clustered together with patches of green cut between sidewalks and streets. People walked just as they had in the mirror. Women wore pants, just as he'd indicated. Their hair ranged in styles and lengths. Katherine glanced at her earasaid. No one else besides Raibeart wore plaid.

She turned her attention to his hands on the wheel. For centuries she'd seen their painted twins and wondered what it would be like to be held by them. She'd stared at his arms, wishing he'd step away from the cold-eyed woman next to him and wrap them around her. She'd wondered what it would feel like to have someone in the bed next to her, a warmth, a presence, a lover, a friend.

She reached slowly for his hand on the wheel and let it hover. When her fingers came close, pain vibrated up her arm in warning, stinging her like a thousand knives peeling away the flesh. His fingers lifted and he angled his hand toward her as if inviting her to touch him.

She snatched her hand back and the pain went away, leaving her numb.

"None of this feels real. Am I dreaming?" she whispered.

"No, lassie. This world is as real as any other."

She spotted a man in a kilt outside a building that read "Post Office" and sat up straighter.

"That's Erik, my nephew," Raibeart said. "He lives near the manor with his wife. She runs a business called Love Potions."

"She's a witch?" Katherine turned her head to watch Erik as he stopped to talk to a group of women.

"Human. Green witch. She concocts shampoos and lotions. I'm friends with her ghost grandmother."

Katherine frowned. Ghost?

"Now there is a dead woman who knows how to live better than the living," he continued. "Just keep out of her moonshine. It had me wandering the forest thinking I led an army of trees to fight fishermen. When I sobered up three days later, I was covered in bark and moss. We now have rumors of the Mossman of Wisconsin. There's a blurry picture on the internet with a website, and one of those paranormal hunter television shows is even coming to try to capture me on film. If they're nice laddies, I might help their ratings and make a reappearance."

Raibeart chuckled to himself.

"Cait and Margareta would hate that," he said.

"Do ya have more family here?" Katherine was jealous even as she waited for the answer. She had no one.

"Aye. My brothers Angus, Fergus, and Murdoch technically live in the mansion with their wives, Margareta, Donna, and Cait. They do a lot of traveling with the family businesses. My nephew Kenneth and his wife and their daughter, Jewel, also live there. Jewel is the sweetest angel ya will ever meet. Ya know the saying it takes a village to raise a child. Well, it takes a clan of warlocks to raise a phoenix."

"I don't know what that means." Katherine heard the affection in his softening voice.

His hands dropped from the wheel, but the car kept moving as it steered itself. "Jewel's birth ma was a phoenix and killed herself to pass on her powers to end her immortality. Phoenixes are blessed with unlimited powers, but those powers can also burn them out like a piece of kindling. They burst into flames and regenerate as babies, never the exact same as before. Jewel has never made it to her teen years."

Katherine studied his face carefully, seeing the narrowing of his eyes as if he held back emotion. "Sounds nice to have all your family in the same home."

"Euann and Cora live there as well," he resumed. "But Bruce, Maura, and her husband Curtis all choose to stay in the Hotel Motel in town, which the family owns. Iain moved in with Jane to an apartment above her plant nursery. Erik lives in the other house on the MacGregor hill, the small Victorian his wife inherited. I'd list each relative, but we'd be in this car all day."

"What about children?" She'd seen how his face changed when he talked about Jewel. "Are ya a da?"

"I care deeply for three wee girls, though I have not had children of my own. Jewel, whom I mentioned. Baby Abby came to me by way of a time loop caused by a dhampir curse. She and Jewel played together. I watched her when her people could not. And Abby's great-granddaughter, who has yet to be born but whom I plan on naming Raibeartina. I have not told Maura and Curtis their baby's name yet, but one tiny spell when the nurse fills out the paperwork will make it so when she comes into this world in a few months."

"Baby Abby is the great-grandmother of…." Katherine shook her head, not bothering to work out the time loop timeline of the MacGregor family tree. "I never had children. I can't remember if I wanted them. I think I did."

"I love children. I want a million of them. They're innocent and derive the purest joy from the simplest things. That is a real magick that should be protected at all costs. They don't complicate things like adults." He grinned and put his hands back on the wheel as if pretending to drive as the car took them to the front of a long building. "The same goes for my surprise for ya. It's inside."

"What I need is here?" Katherine looked at the glass door to the building. The car quieted.

"Aye.

"What is—?"

The sound of the car door cut off her question. Raibeart ran around the back of the vehicle and opened her door for her. She stepped out onto the sidewalk. She heard a bark echoing, followed by the purr of a distant car. The bark reminded her of the goat outside the cottage. She'd listened to the bleating, but no matter how hard she looked for it, she could never find the animal.

"This is a place that holds the best kind of magick," Raibeart explained. He started to offer his arm but then pulled back as if a painful sting made him think better of it. "Trust me."

Trust.

Logically, Katherine wasn't sure she should trust him. His image had been in her prison. Yet, something inside her whispered that she could. Nothing about his demeanor caused alarm. He had a charming, playful smile and an easy way of talking. Sure, some of what he said made little sense to her, but that was to be expected in this futuristic world.

She supposed it was possible that her judgment of who was safe and who was not had become impaired over time. Hundreds of years alone had done their damage. Maybe none of it mattered. She'd been ready to die to end it. No torture could be worse than the isolation she'd been living in.

Raibeart guided her into the building. She expected to see a sparkling magick shooting through the air. Instead, they were greeted by a strange creature through a window cut out who stood guard over a small entryway. She had long black hair and a face coated in white powder. Dark smudges lined her eyes, and silver spikes protruded from her wrist and neck. Rings lined an eyebrow and hung from the nose.

"What manner of creature is that?" Katherine whispered.

"She's goth," Raibeart answered. "Hi, Crow."

"What up, Rai? What up, Rai's date?" Crow greeted with a smile. Her lips were also painted black.

Katherine looked at the ceiling. There was nothing of note over them.

The goth disappeared, only to reappear opening the door to let them inside.

"How're the guests?" Raibeart asked.

"Excitable," Crow answered. "We got a new intake. Little werewolf is having a hard time adjusting. He could probably use some of that whatever-it-is that you do."

"Ya take in werewolf children?" Katherine asked.

Crow laughed.

"We'll be in the garden," Raibeart said.

"Sure thing, boss." Crow saluted and turned to go back to her guard post behind the desk.

"One second." Raibeart lifted a hand to touch Crow's cheek and stopped her. He stared at her for a long moment. "You're getting a raise, and we're putting in a daycare. All will be well this time."

Crow touched her stomach and looked surprised. "The doctor said after…that I couldn't…"

Raibeart smiled. "After all the good ya put into this world, some of it was bound to return to ya."

Crow slowly nodded and returned to her post.

Katherine put her hand over her nose as she followed Raibeart down a hallway. "What's that smell?"

"Bleach." He wound through a couple of hallways.

As they passed a door with a tiny window, she

pecked inside. Kittens played and pounced over a jungle of cat trees. A group of children sat amongst them, giggling as the fluffy animals pretended to attack.

"Is this a sanctuary?" Katherine asked.

"Animal shelter." Raibeart stopped at a glass door overlooking the outside. Dogs ran over a beautiful garden area set up just for them. Paths for running were filled with obstacles. Tunnels and pools provided distractions. Several dogs even rested under the shade of a tree.

"I don't think I understand," Katherine said.

A small dog ran circles around her larger counterparts, herding them together before running them down the path. Katherine couldn't help smiling.

"The best magick." Raibeart grinned. "Unconditional love."

"But...?" Katherine didn't know how this was supposed to help her.

"Ya have been living alone for a long time without physical contact. For some reason, painful magick is keeping me from ya. I saw how ya flinched when Cait tried to touch your arm, but it didn't seem to hurt ya as much as make ya uncomfortable. So..." He gestured outside at the garden. "This is my favorite place on Earth. A paradise of unconditional love.

They don't judge. All they want from ya is love in return."

"Here's the new guy." Crow appeared carrying a squirming bundle of brown fur in her arms. "Poor thing is a little skittish. We think someone left him on the side of the interstate. A driver found him and brought him in."

"Och, is this the new little werewolf to our pack?" Raibeart reached for the dog and carried him outside. "Come on, laddie. Let's make some friends, shall we? I promise ya it will all be well."

Katherine watched him through the door. Raibeart held the animal against his chest and danced as dogs ran up excited to see him. The door muffled the sound of his singing.

"This world is strange," Katherine whispered to herself.

"Are you like a cousin or something?" Crow asked when Raibeart was well into the animal garden.

Katherine shook her head. She tried not to stare at the metal spikes around the girl's neck. "No. We're not related. I barely know him."

"Anytime we see a kilt in town, we assume it's another MacGregor."

Katherine glanced down at her dress.

"You know Rai built this whole place," Crow said, leaning against the door to watch Raibeart walk the new dog around the garden and hold him up to some of the current residents. "He designed it, brought in the best vets, made the shelter no-kill, and never turns away an animal in need. He also insists on talking to anyone who wishes to adopt a pet. Plus, he gave me a job after only one question, with no judgment. I'm sure it's no surprise people around here tend to judge a book by its cover, and my cover is, well... let's just say not many people read my genre."

"Why are ya telling me this?"

Crow nodded to where Raibeart held a conversation with a pack of dogs. They sat around him, heads tilted as if they listened.

"Because he's a good man and one of the few people in this world whom I think deserves more than they've been given. I know he's odd. Sometimes he says things that make little sense on the surface. And I know he asks every woman he meets to marry him, but his heart is in the right place. Being like everyone else is overrated. You know, for what it's worth." Crow turned to leave. "I need to watch the front desk."

Katherine looked back out at Raibeart with the dogs. He smiled and waved her to join them.

She hesitated before going outside.

"I told them all about ya," Raibeart motioned to his audience. "They promise to behave."

The dogs stood and walked toward her one by one, tails wagging. The first nudged her hand. Katherine slowly touched its soft head. The contact mesmerized her after being alone for so long. A second pressed his warm head into her free hand. Within moments she found herself on the ground, surrounded by eager friends. The little werewolf newcomer hopped onto her lap.

Raibeart appeared above them and nodded in approval. "See. Pure magick."

Chapter Eight

Raibeart saw the lightening of Katherine's spirit during the visit to the animal shelter. After hours with the dogs, she'd spent time in the cat room. Sometimes all a person needed was the simplest, most ordinary magick, no spells or potions, just time and uncomplicated affection.

He drove back to the manor slowly, not caring that it aggravated other drivers. She didn't hug her knees to her chest this time and appeared more relaxed.

Raibeart felt his magick building without him willing it to do so. It pulled from the forest as he drove up the long drive to the MacGregor mansion. By the time he reached the top, it was spilling out of him onto Katherine.

She took a deep breath and looked at him in surprise. "This world is becoming clearer."

"Do ya remember anything more about your prison?"

She shook her head in denial. "But I now know what a vet does."

Raibeart didn't bother parking Euann's car in the garage. This wasn't the first time he'd borrowed it without asking.

Once inside the house, Katherine seemed mesmerized by the foyer chandelier and sweeping staircase. She stared at the tiny sliver of daylight reflecting on the floor.

Voices came from the dining room, sounding like a family meeting.

"Ya say the word, and we'll run," Raibeart whispered.

"What word?"

He grinned. "Run."

Katherine nodded.

Raibeart led her to the dining room. His nephews and nieces were gathered with his brothers and sisters. Clearing his throat for their attention, he said, "This is Katherine. I've given her sanctuary here." He pointed around the table, "Euann, Erik, Bruce, Maura, Uncle Chicken, Angus, Margareta, Murdoch, and ya know Cait."

"Uncle Chicken?" Katherine looked confused.

"Iain," Iain corrected.

"He's a bird shifter," Raibeart explained.

"Oh, ah—" Katherine stared at Iain in surprise.

"Hey—" Iain began in protest.

"It's fine. She knows all about magick, don't ya?" Raibeart glanced at Katherine.

She nodded. "I met a goth today."

Erik and Euann laughed. Bruce smiled as he picked at a dried smudge of green paint on his arm. Maura leaned back in her chair with her hand on her pregnant stomach, looking like she'd rather be in bed. Carrying a dhampir's baby demanded a very delicate balance of magick.

"That's the new baby I was telling ya about," Raibeart said, motioning to Maura's stomach.

Raibeartina," Katherine said, showing she remembered.

"Raibeart-what?" Maura sat up a little straighter.

Raibeart waved away the question.

"Crow isn't magickal," Cait stated. "She's human, and like most humans, she shouldn't know about the paranormal."

"Crow doesn't," Raibeart stated. "Katherine does."

Katherine inched behind him a little as if to

hide from their stares. "I think I'm human. Or I was."

"Can ya wield magick?" Euann asked. "Cast spells?"

She shook her head in denial.

"Turn into another creature?" Erik leaned forward to get a better look.

Again, Katherine shook her head.

"Then why do ya doubt your humanity?" Bruce asked.

"I lived in a cottage by myself for hundreds of years under some kind of curse," she answered.

"Brutal," Bruce acknowledged.

"It's a good thing ya found us," Maura said. "We have a little bit of experience with breaking curses."

"Are ya joining us for the meeting?" Angus asked.

"We need your business reports," Margareta said. "It's been months."

"Oh, aye." Raibeart often spaced off the MacGregor family business meetings. If he needed to tell his family something, he would.

"Should we talk about any of that now?" Euann nodded toward Katherine.

"I vouch for her," Raibeart said. He started his report before anyone could protest. "I'm adding a daycare to the animal shelter for employees. I cast syphilis spells on some politicians who were blocking our food donation supply chains overseas. I stole a Michigan man's dog and relocated him to a nice home in Colorado. We own a puppet show. Cora and I are building a banned book section in the library."

"How does the Michigan dog count as business?" Erik asked.

"The dog needed help. I made it my business." Raibeart snorted at the obvious answer. "The tech company is giving away smartphones to rural areas overseas, and we're footing the bill. The chef program in New York's homeless shelter started rocky. The French arsehole tried to feed snails to—*oh*, and I took five hundred million out of the account to pay for the new MacGregor Women's Health Clinics. Fuck politics. Ya don't mess with my ladies. That's my report."

"Wait, so the French chef served snails to the homeless?" Euann clarified.

"No." Raibeart waved off his nephew's pointless question. "I said he *tried*."

"I don't suppose ya put any of that in a spreadsheet?" Margareta asked.

Raibeart laughed as he went toward the kitchen. "I'm setting Katherine up in my room. She's staying as long as she likes."

Cait grabbed a tray of pastries off the table

and held it toward Katherine. "Raibeart sometimes forgets to stop and eat. Here, take one."

Katherine took a cheese Danish and nodded her thanks.

"Do ya know what's strange?" Cait said when they were out of the room. "I don't think he asked this one to marry him."

"That can't be right. Unless that one is married, he probably did it when ya weren't listening," Angus answered.

"Should we be worried about this? Do ya think it's a coincidence that he showed up this morning bloody, moments before her arrival?" Margareta asked.

Raibeart ignored his family's fretting.

Katherine sniffed the Danish and then held it out to Raibeart. "I don't think I want this. Ya said not to eat anything Cait gave me."

"Oh, aye." He reached to take it.

"And thank ya for—"

Raibeart's hand accidentally bumped Katherine's finger as he tried to take the Danish. She inhaled sharply in pain. Her eyes rounded in fright. Ice-cold agony shot up his arm.

Katherine vanished. The Danish fell to the floor.

The cold traveled like death over him, stopping his magick from flowing as a white mist filled his vision. He did not want to go into the fog, but it did not give him a choice. Death was one force that was hard to stop.

Raibeart found himself standing alone in the Highlands of his younger days. The cold stayed inside him, making it difficult to move. Numbing pain centered in his chest.

Was this the afterlife?

Was it a dream?

He looked at his hands. They did not appear of the ethereal realm to him, but then he knew that ghosts did not always realize they were ghosts.

Was this how a warlock died? By a single touch in the family kitchen?

"Katherine!" he yelled.

She had disappeared too. What afterlife had she gone to?

"Show me," he whispered, willing his magick to light the way to her.

Raibeart felt his powers trying to stir, but they fizzled before anything happened.

He forced his legs to move as he searched for her. The sunlight shifted and changed as if hours had passed in seconds. He didn't know which direction to go. Helpless without his magick, Raibeart cried out in frustration. Snow began to fall, and his powerless body was ill-equipped to deal with the dropping temperature.

"She knows you betrayed her," a disembodied voice whispered. The English accent was not familiar. "She died with that knowledge in her heart."

"I didn't betray anyone," Raibeart denied. "Show yourself, demon."

"Poor Raibeart, desperately searching for something he'll never find, for I have her locked away." The woman laughed, a cold sound that belied the prettiness of her voice.

"Who are ya?" he demanded.

"You refused to give me everything I wanted, so I took everything you had in return. How does eternity feel, my love? Endlessly searching and waiting for something you can't have."

"What are ya talking about, ya deceitful hell spawn?"

"You're hurting my feelings, lover." The voice seemed to move, now coming from behind. "I never lied to you. It is you who were deceitful. You made me give you my love, but you never returned it. You can't play with people like that, Raibeart."

"Show your face, coward," he demanded.

"You want to see something?" the woman chuckled. "Look."

Raibeart turned. In the distance, a cottage built in the Tudor style had appeared. A feeling of desperation surged inside him. He hurried toward it, running as fast as he could on frozen legs. The crunch of snow beneath his boots echoed over the foggy landscape.

Lights flickered in the window as if inviting him inside. The solitary bleating of a goat came over the distance. In his heart, he knew what this place was. An aura of pain pulsed around the cottage like a beacon of warning.

"Katherine!" he yelled, eager to find her.

He pushed harder, swinging his arms for momentum. He reached the door and tried to jerk it open, but it was sealed shut. Hurrying to a window, he peeked inside. Katherine stood on a chair and threaded a rope over her head. He pounded on the window to get her attention. She didn't hear him.

He saw the agony on her face as she kicked the chair free. Raibeart grunted and had to look away as her feet swung. When he forced his eyes back, she was no longer hanging. Instead, she was mid-thrust, stabbing herself in the stomach. Wild eyes didn't appear to see him even though they looked in his direction. Her hair had been cut and sprinkled around her on the floor. Katherine cried out in pain, doubling over.

"Stop it!" Raibeart yelled.

A face reflected in the window as if the

tormenting woman stood behind him. Her dark hair and eyes were unfamiliar, yet she seemed to know him. He glanced back, but no one was there. "These are my favorite moments. Collected from a stopped clock. Don't you like them?"

The roar of fire came from within, and he felt the heat as the inside of the cottage went up in flames. He didn't try to run as he struck the window to get inside. The glass cracked but instantly healed.

"Katherine!"

"Katherine, Katherine," the woman mocked with a laugh.

Raibeart ran for the door and kicked it as hard as he could. The action jarred his ankle, but it forced the door open. He ran inside as smoke billowed out.

Once he made it inside, the fire instantly dissipated. The small room was set up as if staged and waiting for a guest. He felt Katherine's presence within her prison world. It called to him.

"Katherine?" Raibeart searched for her, hurrying down a hallway. He passed a mirror, and the movement caused him to back up and look inside. In the reflection, he watched his family search for him through the house and back gardens like a television show.

Raibeart ignored the mirror and jabbed his

shoulder into a door, flinging it open in his haste. He found himself in his bedroom, standing before his red comforter on an empty bed. A fire burned in the fireplace underneath a portrait of him standing with the woman whose reflection he'd seen in the glass. Dressed like a noblewoman, she hung on his arm like she belonged there. Feeling fingers creeping around his biceps, he slapped the sensation to stop it.

A soft rustle came from the bed as two shadowy figures appeared to be making love.

"Don't you remember us?" the woman purred.

Raibeart frowned and refused to look at the bed. He heard the evil woman moving behind him.

"Where is Katherine?" Raibeart went to look for her.

"You hurt my feelings, Raibeart." The woman appeared before he could leave, blocking him. Her eyes narrowed, and she grabbed hold of his shoulders.

Raibeart felt her sucking the energy from him. He tried to push her away, but she was too strong. He fell to his knees. Her eyes glowed as she siphoned his trapped magick.

"Do you know me now?"

"Inthrall," he answered.

"I prefer Alice." She leaned over and kissed his forehead as if unlocking old memories.

He had only met her once centuries ago, but he recognized the feeling of his magick being forced out of his body. According to his family, Raibeart's inthrall was responsible for leaving him a broken, crazy bachelor. He had barely remembered that night. They claimed that before meeting this creature, he'd been reasonably normal.

Inthralls were humans and were generally known as the suckerfish of the supernatural world. Just one touch and they could suck the life force from their targets and leave them for dead. Usually, it had to be the right combination of human and warlock for the transfer of power to work. Such a person was rare and wouldn't be able to feed off just any warlock.

As the memories unfolded, he said, "I remember I got drunk after a battle and dropped my guard. We'd lost a good number of men that night. Ya seduced me and stole my magick."

The night itself was not remarkable after centuries of living, so he wasn't surprised he'd forgotten Alice.

"Don't play the victim," Alice scolded. "You can't seduce a man who doesn't want to be seduced. Stop lying to yourself. You know what we have is special."

"Aye," he admitted. She started to smile. "Special like the black horse of the Apocalypse. There might only be one, but no one wants to take the diseased beast for a ride."

Alice's expression fell, and her eyes narrowed in rage. She began screeching and swinging her arms to strike him. Raibeart pressed his palms against his ears. The pain of her wail radiated to his bones. No human should have been able to make such a noise, but after centuries of feeding on his magick and simmering in rage, she'd turned into something dark and powerful.

How could he not have realized Alice's connection to him before now?

Tears rolled down his face, and he wanted to claw the eardrums from his head to get the noise to stop.

Alice quieted and dropped to her knees to face him. She breathed heavily, looking exhausted, as she grabbed hold of his face. "I don't know how you got her out, but I'm going to take her away from you to a place you will never find her. She is going to suffer worse than before for what you denied me. And you're going to know it was your magick that made it possible. She can't have your love, Raibeart. That's mine. It's always been mine."

Raibeart reached to jerk her hands from his face. Her fingertips pinched into his skin like icicles, clawing his flesh. The moment his right palm met her wrist, she screamed and jerked away from him. Her body was propelled backward, carried by an unseen force as the cottage room disappeared, and she dissipated into the dreamy mist that clung to the landscape.

Raibeart's hand throbbed. He'd forgotten about the mystical burn. The spot had begun to turn an angry red around the wound.

He rubbed the tears from his cheek only to find that they weren't tears but blood trails.

When he thought of his life, he saw puzzle pieces scattered around. In the ones that fit together, images of his family smiled back at him. He saw the animal shelter and the numerous charities. He saw the things that were most important to him.

But now he also saw Alice.

She had been there most of his life, haunting him, feeding off him, always hidden in the shadows. She was the drunken crone in the tavern who had told him he needed to look harder for love, the reason he'd started asking every single woman to marry him. She'd planted that seed of desperation inside of him. That search had distracted his attention so that she could feed.

The empty spaces, the ones whose pieces were lost, now had a name. Katherine. Raibeart couldn't remember what had happened between them; only, according to Alice, he had loved Katherine.

Her name called to him. *Katherine. Bonnie sweet Katherine.*

How could he have forgotten her?

"I'm going to take her away from you to a place you will never find her. She is going to suffer worse than before for what you denied me. And you're going to know it was your magick that made it possible. She can't have your love, Raibeart. That's mine. It's always been mine."

Raibeart tried to push to his feet, but he stumbled. Alice had stolen his energy. He fell against the ground, consumed by the growing mist.

"Da, get up."

Raibeart blinked but was unable to move. A firm hand gripped his shoulder. He couldn't see who spoke.

"Ya need to get out of here before she wakes back up. It's not safe. She has too much power in this place."

Chapter Nine

"Raibeart?" Katherine yelled, spinning around in the forest as she tried to determine which way to go. Mist crept over the ground as if reaching for her. She ran from whatever traveled within the billowing folds.

Raibeart had touched her. Behind the intense agony of the physical contact stirred something familiar. In her panic at being alone, he was the only one she could think to run to. She felt safe with him and was drawn to his kindness.

If this was a new torment, it was worse than centuries of living alone. She'd been given a few hours of compassion and company. If that was taken away....

Tears filled her eyes and burned her nose as she tried to hold them back.

If she were chased back into the cottage with these new memories in her head, the agony would be too much to bear.

"Raibeart?" she whispered. "Are ya out here?"

He'd found her in the forest before. She prayed that he could find her again.

The mist caught up to her, and she turned to face it, raising her arms as it surrounded her. "Who's doing this? Why? What did I do to ya? What did I do?"

"There ya are," a voice came from within the mist.

"Raibeart?" she asked.

"Donovan," the man corrected, appearing before her. "We've been looking for ya ever since ya got out of the cottage."

"We?" She didn't see anyone else.

"Ya shouldn't be here. It's not safe." Donovan took her gently by the elbow and began walking quickly through the mist.

Katherine pulled away from him. "No. I won't go back to the cottage."

"Why would I take ya back? I helped get ya out. Now hurry. We have to go before Alice finds ya," he insisted.

"Who are ya?" Katherine wasn't sure she should go with the man, but the forest presented little choice.

"That is a difficult story." Donovan suddenly stopped. "I thought we'd have more time. She's here."

"Who?" Katherine asked.

"Listen. This is important. My brother and I snuck a loophole into your curse. The only way to escape the curse of the cottage is to be completely broken. Ya must have given up hope. Get it back. Don't give up." Donovan pointed. "Now, run that way. Don't stop, no matter what ya hear."

Katherine hesitated. Donovan gave her a shove before running back the way they had come. She stumbled, and by the time she righted herself, he'd disappeared into the mist.

A loud screech rang out.

"Donovan?" She started to go after him, unsure what she would do if she found him. It didn't feel right, leaving him to fight whatever it was alone.

"Dammit, run!" The man's voice ordered. "I can't hold her off long."

"Come with me," Katherine insisted. "I can't leave ya here."

"She doesn't want to hurt *me*," Donovan screamed. "Go! Before she changes her mind and comes after both of us."

Katherine again hesitated before finally starting to run. She had a hard time seeing where her feet landed on the uneven forest floor as the mist concealed the trail. She aimed for the break in the trees to show her where the path led.

The screeches continued, followed by the sounds of a struggle.

Her heart hammered violently. Fear welled inside her at the unknown. This forest was nothing like her prison. Blue lights shot into the air, exploding overhead. Katherine screamed, ducking for cover with her arms lifted over her head.

The light dissolved, and she found herself huddled on the ground. Her hand bled though she didn't know how she'd injured it.

"Run," she ordered her legs. The whisper barely left her throat.

Katherine somehow managed to force her body upright. She bit back her tears. Her shaking limbs carried her stumbling forward, but not as fast as before. She swung her arm back and forth in the fog, trying to clear it.

For so long, whenever she fantasized about escape, she had thought leaving the cottage would mean freedom, reprieve, relief. She never dreamed her situation could be worse than the endless banality of solitude.

Her swinging hand hit branches. Twigs broke off at the force of her blow. She kept going, blindly fighting the unseeable path. The screeches appeared to come from another direction.

"What did I do?" she whispered into the endless mist.

Was this her new eternity? Running through a forest chased by a creature she could not see?

Katherine punched to the side. Her forearm made contact with flesh.

"Oof," a woman grunted. "What the…?"

Katherine instantly changed course. She ran into a chest. The impact caused her to yelp in surprise.

"Easy." Hands found her arms. The mist withdrew, leaving her standing in the MacGregor's back garden with Cait and Murdoch.

Cait rubbed her shoulder where Katherine had hit her.

"Were ya making all that noise?" Murdoch asked. The screeching had dissipated with the mist.

Katherine shook her head. The fog clung to the surrounding trees like a warning not to enter the woods.

"Where's Raibeart?" Cait asked.

"I don't know," Katherine gestured behind her. "But Donovan is still in there."

"Donovan?" Cait frowned.

"Aye. He told me to run and pointed the way

here." Katherine started moving back toward the trees. "We need to help him. That creature is in there with him."

"Who's Donovan?" Cait asked her husband.

"I knew a few in the old country," Murdoch said. "None who would still be alive today."

The distant echo of the screeching came from the woods. Katherine stopped her charge into the woods and backed up.

"I don't think this is one of Raibeart's drunken games," Cait said. "We may have a bigger problem than we realized."

"Come inside, lassie." Murdoch didn't give her much choice as he stepped around her to shepherd her toward the mansion. "I think it's time ya told us why ya need protection."

"We need to find Raibeart," Katherine said. "He was with me, but then I..."

Cait went ahead of them to open the back door.

"...I appeared in the forest," she finished weakly. She touched her finger where he'd bumped into her hand. "And I don't know what happened to him."

"I saw ya both disappear from the kitchen," Cait said.

"Doesn't that mean he's in the forest?"

Katherine insisted. She knew what it felt like to be lost and alone. "Shouldn't we look?"

"You're the only one we were able to detect in the trees," Cait answered.

"My brother can watch after himself." Murdoch tried to appear reassuring but worry lined his narrowed eyes. "If ya want to help him, then it's best ya tell us everything ya know. What exactly are we up against here?"

Chapter Ten

"Have we met before, Gregory? Ya seem familiar."
Raibeart kept a watchful eye on his travel
companion. The poor lad appeared a few sips
short of a full bottle and insisted on calling
Raibeart his da.

Though they kept a fast pace, there didn't
seem to be an end to the misty terrain. The land
felt dead. His magick had nowhere to pull from
except Gregory, and killing the man for a bit of
power hardly felt right.

"Aye. Hundreds of times, Da," Gregory
answered. "At least this time ya are wearing
clothes."

"I'm sorry, but I'm not your da." Raibeart
watched his feet for several steps. "Who was
your ma?"

"That's a complicated question," Gregory said.

Raibeart chuckled. "Doesn't look like we're going to arrive anywhere anytime soon. I think ya have time to give a complicated answer."

"I have two mas," Gregory said.

"Oh," Raibeart waved a hand in dismissal. "That's naught to be ashamed of."

"I'm not ashamed of anything," Gregory answered.

"Ah." Raibeart nodded in understanding. "Ya were cooked up in one of my fertility clinics. That is why ya call me your da." He grinned. "I like that idea. I'd have to have, what? Few thousand bairns by those standards. That's a lot of birthdays. Maybe I can trick Cait into helping with the shoppin'."

"No."

"Turkey baster deposit from that sperm clinic I bought in the seventies? I didn't make any donations, but those college laddies were excited for the job. If memory serves, ya might not want to look up your real da. I don't think some of them were on their way to graduating with honors, if ya know what I'm sayin'."

"No, not a sperm bank."

"Then you're going to have to help me out. I would remember impregnating a woman the old-fashioned way." Raibeart stopped walking and put his hands on his hips. "Were ya adopted?"

"I wouldn't call it that." Gregory kept walking.

"Well, if I'm your da, I demand ya tell me at once. The whole story."

Gregory laughed. "Why does it matter? Ya never remember the conversation when I do tell ya."

Raibeart lifted his hand, zapping a little energy from the man to make him stumble. The transfer of power was slight and hardly worth noting. This place of anti-magick was beginning to trouble him. The laughter stopped.

Gregory turned to him in annoyance. "My twin brother Donovan and I were stolen from our pregnant ma and put into another ma. She had us and realized she didn't care for raising babies. She then sent us away to live with our first ma's parents until we'd passed our annoying years."

"See, perfectly normal explanation. That wasn't very complicated at all." Raibeart strode faster than before. "What are ya standing around for? Let's find a way out of here."

"How is that perfectly normal?" Gregory rushed to catch up. "We were stolen from one womb and put into another."

"Well, aye, that part is a little unusual,"

Raibeart admitted. "I meant the living with grandparents is perfectly normal."

"A little unusual?" Gregory repeated.

"It would be really strange if ya were moved from your first ma into a goat. Noblewomen attempting to keep their figures tried that for a spell. Ended up with a barnyard full of satyrs."

"I don't think that's true," Gregory denied.

"Can't prove that it isn't." Raibeart quipped. "Some stories are more interesting true rather than not, so ya might as well believe them."

"Ya get this isn't entertainment, right?" Gregory gestured at the endless mist. "Ya get where we are, don't ya?"

"Looks like Scotland."

"If Hell were a realm, this is the doorway," Gregory said.

"That's not a very nice thing to say about Scotland."

"We're not in Scotland." Gregory sighed in frustration. "Alice kept Katherine locked up here. Some demon gave her a key to the place. I'm trying to find the way out. If ya see a cottage or hear a goat, go the opposite direction."

"Ya know Katherine? Is she harmed?" Raibeart grabbed his arm. "Where is she? Take me to her."

Gregory jerked his arm free. "I would have

thought it was obvious. Katherine equals our first ma. Evil bitch aka Alice equals our second ma. Alice trapped Katherine and stole her babies. Congratulations. You're a daddy."

"So ya think Katherine and I…?"

"Aye. Ya had sex. That's normally how babies happen." Gregory glanced back and forth. He lifted his hand, palm out, and then suddenly turned to the right.

"I was going to say, so ya think Katherine and I got married."

"No. Ya didn't do that." Gregory dropped his hand.

"Then ya were told wrong. I would never get a woman pregnant without marrying her first."

Gregory looked around, distracted. "I don't know if ya know this, but ya don't have to be married to have sex."

Raibeart was having a hard time believing the man. "I would have remembered all this."

"Fine. I'm wrong. What do I know? It's only my life."

"I don't think this is Hell's doorway." Raibeart leaned over to grab a rock from the ground. He held it firmly in his fist. "I've felt evil."

"Ya know what they say about the devil's greatest trick…."

Raibeart laughed. "Making fried foods delicious and then telling humans they have to eat carrots instead?"

"Convincing ya he doesn't exist," Gregory corrected.

"I think the fried food thing is meaner." Raibeart's laughter died. "Speaking of which, I was supposed to go with the family to the Crimson Tavern tonight for loaded tater tot nachos. Any chance we can wrap this adventure up soon?"

"Gee, Da, it's great to spend time with ya too," Gregory drawled sarcastically.

The rock in Raibeart's hand began to vibrate and smoke. The putrid fumes enveloped his fingers.

"Sulfur?" He wrinkled his nose and tossed the rock away. Maybe Gregory did know what he was talking about, and this was some sort of Hell realm.

"Alice's calling card," Gregory corrected.

A distant scream sounded.

"And she's in a mood." Gregory visibly stiffened.

Raibeart's ears ached in protest, and he covered them. "Her song's worse than a banshee's wail."

"And can be twice as deadly." Gregory didn't appear to be as affected by the noise. Seeing Raibeart watching him, he said, "My brother and

I grew up with it. We developed a natural immunity."

Gregory reached into his pocket and pulled out a small pouch. He dumped a stone into his hand and tossed it toward Raibeart. "Here. Hold this."

As he caught it, Raibeart had a flash of déjà vu. He recalled catching a similar object on multiple occasions. It was the same size as the burn on his hand.

"We've been here before." Raibeart had a cloudy vision of Gregory and his twin.

"Here? No."

He pinched the stone between his fingers and held it up. "I remember seeing this."

"It keeps her from killing ya." Gregory looked up at the sky as the screams grew louder. "But the magick burns out, so we must keep replacing it. Since ya never remember us, it's this conversation over and over again. I have to tell ya, Da, there have been times when we've considered just letting this family drama play itself out."

The screeching grew louder, but Raibeart's pain lessened as he held the stone. His fist clenched around it, unable to open.

"Next time, we might not have a choice." Gregory looked sad. "That's the last of our protection stones. They're not easy to come by. We only got these because we helped a troll trapped in a mine."

Raibeart frowned. "How long have ya been saving my life?"

"The first time was in the early 1700s. Back then, the rages weren't as frequent as they are now or as bad. Alice had approached ya in a tavern and wasn't happy when ya didn't leave with her."

Raibeart felt blood trailing from his nose and swiped at it. "Ya should stay behind me. I don't have magick here to help us. If she comes, I'll distract her while ya run to safety."

The mist parted, and a figure propelled toward them. Alice glowed with red, casting an eerie light over Gregory's face. Her mouth was open wide as the rage poured out of her. Her eyes were wild.

"Alice, stop!" Gregory stepped in front of him.

"Out of the way, laddie," Raibeart ordered, shoving him aside.

Alice hovered inches from Raibeart's face, screaming at him. The pain became unbearable, yet he somehow managed to keep on his feet. He closed his eyes, feeling the warm tears streaking down his cheeks.

Like this, Alice's beauty had faded. All that was left was the insanity of her rage. She stopped screaming and simply stared at him, chest heaving with breaths, eyes swirling with fire. The red glow lessened but not enough to put them out of danger.

"Alice. I don't know why this happened to ya, but...." Raibeart lifted his fist with the stone and touched her cheek. The magick burned into his palm as Alice's renewed scream was cut off. She was thrust back as quickly as she arrived, leaving red smoke in her wake.

"Time to go." Gregory grabbed hold of his arm and tugged him into Alice's trail.

They stumbled into the MacGregor's kitchen, right where Raibeart had been when he'd been sucked into Alice's world. Raibeart coughed the red sulfur from his lungs as he shook his twice-burned palm.

Gregory took one deep breath and lowered his head as he let it out with a sigh. The man looked weary from fighting an endless battle.

"Raibeart?" Margareta appeared in the doorway. "What happened? Where have ya been?"

"That's my cue. Until the next time, Da." Gregory didn't acknowledge Margareta as he moved to leave through the door opposite her entrance.

"Da?" Margareta demanded.

Gregory's head whipped around to stare at her.

Margareta placed her hands on her hips and eyed Gregory. "Why is this man calling ya Da?"

"Ya can see me?" Gregory sounded shocked.

"Of course, I can. Ya are standing in my kitchen." Margareta quipped. "He must be yours, Raibeart. He talks nonsense just like ya. Why am I just now meeting my nephew?"

"Alice's magick must be cracking. Normally ya can't see us. We tried for years—"

"Donovan?" Katherine entered the kitchen with Murdoch and Cait. Her gaze flittered to Raibeart. "You're safe."

Raibeart didn't think as he crossed over to her. He started to reach for her, and she pulled away. They stared at each other for a moment. Her hand lifted, coming slowly toward him. The pain did not rise as it had before. Their fingers touched.

Katherine sighed deeply in relief. Raibeart felt that small contact throughout his entire body. The urge to hold her became strong. He wanted to carry her out of there and protect her from Alice. Gregory's words could not have convinced him, but that touch did. He had known this woman before. He had touched her skin. He knew what her kiss would feel like. He had seen her naked.

"I'm Gregory." Gregory placed a hand on his chest before reaching for Katherine's shoulder to get her attention. "You've seen my brother Donovan?"

"He was in the forest mist and—" Before Katherine could finish the sentence, Gregory pushed past her and ran from the home.

"What is going on?" Margareta demanded. "Why does Raibeart have a son we don't know about?"

"A son?" Cait demanded.

"Raibeart?" Katherine whispered, staring at him as if she didn't hear the conversation going on around them. "I remember us. I remember…"

"Aye." He nodded. The memories were cloudy but there. After being buried for hundreds of years, it was no surprise they would need time to come into focus.

Anger filled him as he thought of someone taking her face from his memory, but it was soon tempered as he stared at her. Dark emotion had no place inside him when he gazed into her beautiful eyes.

"Family meeting," Margareta ordered loud enough for anyone on the lower level of the house to hear. She pointed at Katherine and Raibeart. "And ya two are going to be the guests of honor. Time to start talking. What is going on here?"

"I told ya bad magick is afoot," Raibeart answered. "Ya never believe me."

Murdoch slapped his brother's shoulder before turning him toward the dining room. "Ya also once told us ya were turning into a leprechaun because your willy had a grass stain."

"No. It was my arse," Raibeart corrected. He grabbed Katherine's hand, intent on not letting her out of his sight.

Chapter Eleven

The MacGregor family meant well.

Katherine could see they cared for their brother, but they sometimes talked to him like he was a child needing direction. Margareta often cut him off mid-sentence, and Cait would shake her head like an exasperated parent. Murdoch and Angus followed them up with jokes, reminding Raibeart of some antic he'd done in the past—running naked and drunk through the woods, getting them lost on some make-believe adventure, proposing to endless women. Raibeart was their fool, and they appeared to enjoy laughing at him.

Katherine also knew that despite these flaws, they needed the family's help and experience. She was not a witch or a warlock, and she did not understand the magick that had kept her locked away for centuries. Before her prison, she had been a young woman with small dreams. She wanted her family safe. She wanted to find a husband to love. She wanted children. She went to church, did her chores, and helped her neighbors whenever it was within her ability.

"Drink more," Cait urged, pouring dark liquid into her cup. "It will help."

Katherine didn't care for the bitter drink, but it did seem to help clear her thoughts. Talking about the past unfurrowed her memories, smoothing out the edges and bringing light to the shadows. Raibeart stayed by her side, holding her hand under the table as if afraid to let go.

"Eat." Margareta put yet another tray of food in front of her, trying to tempt her appetite. Katherine took the only thing that looked familiar —a slice of oat bread with honey. She didn't feel like eating, but it seemed to make Raibeart's sisters happy, so she made an effort.

Katherine held nothing back, telling them everything she remembered. When she finished with her story, Raibeart did the same. Some of what he said was difficult to hear.

She was a mother. They were parents.

Katherine did not remember being pregnant, though she remembered making love like it was a scene watched through the prison mirror. She remembered being happy, but that happiness felt like a dream within a dream held hostage by a nightmare. Still, her desire to protect Donovan in the misty forest had been as strong as it had been confused.

Alice was an inthrall. Raibeart's inthrall.

"She has helped herself to my magick for so long that it has sapped away her sanity. Whatever perceived slight she carries with her is now wrapped up in rage and delusion," Raibeart said.

"Not only her sanity," Murdoch answered. "It is fair to say her thievery has, at times, affected your sanity as well."

"It would explain the nightmares and why ya feel the need to run yourself to sleep each night," Angus added.

"Though it doesn't explain the naked part," Margareta muttered to her husband.

Perhaps the hardest to hear was that Raibeart had betrayed her with Alice. That is how the woman first got hold of his magick.

"That's one hell of an STD," Murdoch whispered to Angus, none too quietly.

Logic told Katherine not to hold a grudge about something that had happened centuries ago. Still, she couldn't help but wonder how life would have gone had he not done it. Alice would never have taken his magick, or their children, or her freedom.

When she looked at Raibeart's face, she saw his guilt. From all accounts, he had been in his own prison of sorts. There was no reason for her to add to his pain.

"I'll talk to Euann and tell him to ensure the supernatural security systems are all in place." Margareta stood. "Alice will not be getting back in here without us knowing about it."

Katherine wanted to point out that Alice hadn't come into the house but had instead brought them to her domain.

"I'll let the rest of the family know," Cait said. "I needed to go through the mirror to order lotions from Lydia for the women's shelter gift bags."

"Now everyone knows everything," Raibeart stated, standing up from his chair. He kept hold of her hand, taking her with him. "Moonlight beckons."

"You're not to leave the house tonight," Cait ordered.

Raibeart threaded his arm through Katherine's and guided her toward his room.

"And get that girl proper clothing. Ya both look like ya crawled out of a Renaissance Faire."

Cait paused. "Raibeart, acknowledge ya hear me."

"Aye, harpie, I hear ya." Raibeart lifted his hand and waved without turning to look at his sister. Lower, so only Katherine could hear him, he said, "They mean well, but with Alice tapped into my magick, there is nowhere for us to hide. This isn't like a siren or succubus. We're all connected. I feel my magick lingering in ya, too. Hiding from her is like trying to hide from ourselves. We can build walls and put on armor, but in the end, we're locked in a room with ourselves. The best we can do is make it so she can't force us to go with her."

"What did she mean 'through the mirror'?" Katherine asked.

"Margareta gave her oldest Erik a portal mirror when he moved out of the house into the Victorian his wife inherited. It's a fast jog away, but ya know mas and their bairns. She's been trying to find more for her other children, but they're not exactly something ya can pick up at the local hardware store."

"In the prison, there was a mirror that could see the outside world. Is that what ya mean? Like that?" she asked.

"That sounds more like a cursed object." Raibeart frowned. "Portals have two sides. Ya can step through portals to get from one place to another. Some are one-way, like a fairy ring. The mirror in Erik's house is two-way."

"The mirror only allowed me to watch the outside world." She took a deep breath. "The memories are becoming stronger now. I think I saw our sons when Alice brought them to my parents. It's almost too painful to think about. Seeing them and not being able to touch them. Not being able to explain what happened to my family."

Raibeart opened his bedroom door.

Katherine peered inside and refused to go in. "It looks exactly like the cottage. I don't want to be in there."

"This is how my bedroom has looked for as long as I can remember," he said. "But I can't recall why. I always had this feeling and kept it to remind me of something I knew I had forgotten."

Shadows began to move on the bed as if two people made love. She felt the stirring in her body at the idea of touching him as it tried to remember the feel of his. Though, something about this bed still felt wrong.

"We didn't make love in a bed," Katherine said, realizing the shadows were not depicting them. She had to look away. The painful thoughts were too unbearable. "I remember the moon above and the air on my skin. We were outside. This wasn't us."

Fingers brushed her cheek. "I'm sorry, Katherine."

She couldn't answer, couldn't say that it was all right or that it didn't matter. It did matter.

"I should have resisted her seduction. It was one time, after a battle. The English had used magick, and I realized it too late. Out of the thirty men who fought with us that day, only two of us lived. We drowned our sorrows in ale until we couldn't move. It's no excuse, though. I should have been stronger."

Katherine fought the irritation that simmered at the thought. Or was it jealousy? The emotion was impossible to name. "I don't know that I want to hear about your time with Alice."

"She drained my magick," he finished. "I woke up disoriented. Somehow, she kept the spicket open and has been stealing power ever since."

"It's over," she snapped. "It happened."

"But I—"

"Raibeart." Katherine tapped his chest. "I don't want to hear about your night with Alice."

"There is barely anything to tell."

"Then stop telling it." Katherine felt his heart beating beneath her hand. The warmth crept into her fingers. Even in her irritation, she liked being next to him.

When she glanced at the bed, the shadowy lovers had disappeared.

"I never meant to hurt ya," he said.

"I believe that." It was the truth. She didn't feel anything malicious or evil in him.

Katherine touched his cheek. Whiskered stubble rubbed against her palm. She touched his bottom lip with her thumb, trying to remember what a kiss felt like.

"We don't have to stay here. This house has more bedrooms than people right now. Ya can take your pick."

"Wait here."

Raibeart looked at the doorway. "Here?"

"Aye." Katherine didn't go into his bedroom but instead went to the room next to his. Inside looked completely different, with a thick salmon, pink, and gray patterned bedspread. She went to the bed and took the covers. Bundling them into her arms, she hurried out of the room. "Ya mentioned something about moonlight?"

"As my lady wishes." Raibeart took the bundle from her.

Instead of escorting her toward the gardens, he led the opposite way down the hall. They walked down a narrow flight of stairs to the basement and then to a small door that opened to the side yard.

The evening air felt crisp in a way that her prison never had. She took a deep breath. The smells of nature differed from Scotland. A hint of floral underlined the moss and earth, with traces of Raibeart when the breeze picked up.

"Through here." Raibeart cut across the yard to a path. They moved through the woods.

After a while, she asked, "Where are we going?"

"I never know for sure, but we'll know when we get there." He adjusted the blanket in his arms. "Are ya frightened?"

"Darkness doesn't scare me. I'm happy to be away from that cottage. And if I'm truthful, away from people. It's a lot of energy and voices. I thought I'd want that, but after solitude…."

"Aye," he said in understanding. They came to a fork in the path, and he stopped. "Which way do ya think?"

"I don't know these woods."

He smiled. "Isn't that a beautiful thing? Pick a path, commit, and trust in the decision, and it will get ya where ya are going."

She realized it was indeed a beautiful thing not to know the path ahead of her while still feeling safe with him next to her. Katherine glanced back and forth before pointing. Raibeart followed her direction. They did it a couple of more times before coming to a clearing.

"Ah, see, perfect." He nodded in approval. "This was just where we were looking for."

Katherine turned slowly to observe their surroundings. "The silence used to drive me mad, all those empty hours. I thought I'd give anything for a room full of voices. Then, sitting with your family, all perfectly nice and lovely people, though I don't like how they talk to ya sometimes, I felt overwhelmed and just wanted a moment of silence again. It's like I'm broken. I don't know who I am."

"The only way to escape the curse of the cottage is to be completely broken. Ya must have given up hope. Get it back. Don't give up."

That was what Donovan had said to her. She needed to get her hope back. But how?

"Broken things can be fixed." Raibeart hummed to himself as he spread the covers on the ground. "It's demolished things that ya have to be wary of."

Raibeart placed his hands on his hips and looked up through the opening in the branches. Stars shone brightly in the clear sky.

"I like to come to the forest because it's always familiar—trees, dirt, sky," he said. "Sometimes I forget what time I'm in, but it doesn't matter in the woods. Most nights, I drink and run myself into exhaustion just to keep the nightmares at bay. I don't feel the need to do that with ya here."

Katherine went toward him. She didn't stop to think as she lifted on her toes to kiss him softly. Her lips met his surprised ones as her hand touched his cheek.

Raibeart instantly returned the kiss, deepening it. He pulled her against him, holding her close. The safety of his strong embrace enveloped her. Worlds faded. This was familiar. It was where they were meant to be.

Hundreds of years melted away like the last tremors of a nightmare. During her solitude, it had felt endless, but now it was as if no time had passed between this kiss and their last.

She remembered the moisture that had been on his face. The rain had wet his hair, and it clung to his shoulders. She'd thought he was insane to have traveled through the foul weather to visit her. But she'd also been so excited to see him.

"The first time I saw ya, ya were carrying a basket from the garden," he whispered against her mouth. "Ya carried yourself like a true Highland queen. It didn't matter that your dress was old and dirt covered your hands. Every sliver of magick in the universe converged in that moment, and I knew I belonged to ya."

Their bodies shifted, rubbing against each other. Her fingers went to his kilt to unfasten the belt. "Ya walked up to me and told me ya were going to ask my father for my hand in marriage."

Raibeart chuckled, the laugh rumbling deep inside his chest. "He said no."

She nodded, remembering. "He had every right to demand ya prove yourself worthy."

"It didn't stop us."

She shook her head in denial. "No. It didn't stop us."

Raibeart swept her into his arms. She heard his kilt fall from the loosened belt. He held her close, gazing into her eyes before slowly lowering her to the ground. He laid her on the covers and came next to her. Running the back of his hand down her chest, he undressed her with his magick. The gown melted off her skin and pooled next to her.

Katherine caressed him in the same way, only his shirt stayed on. "That's hardly fair."

"My magick is at your command." He took her hand in his and repeated the gesture. This time his shirt slithered off his chest. His magick tingled her fingers before traveling down her arm to the rest of her body. It heightened her awareness.

She pulled his head down to meet hers and hooked her leg over his thigh. Her boot hit against him, and she laughed. "Boots?"

Understanding, he waved his hand, and their boots disappeared from their feet.

Her hand roamed down his shoulder, over his arm, before moving to his waist. Warm flesh beckoned her exploring fingers as they glided along his hip and around to a firm ass check. She gripped him tight, pulling him closer.

Her legs move restlessly along his, desperate to feel him. Memories surfaced, mingling with the present. She knew his body, his touch. She wanted him as badly as she had that first time.

Katherine might have forgotten herself for a time in the prison, but one truth emerged. She loved him as much at this moment as she ever had. They had a bond that had withstood time, memory loss, curses, and an evil inthrall. Even when they couldn't remember, it had been there, linking them, just waiting for the moment his magick could pull her from her prison cell back into his arms. She knew this man intimately, instinctively.

"She tried to take everything from us." Katherine attempted to fight the emotions, but the sexual energy was too strong. "She made me forget ya."

"Our love will outlast any curse." When Raibeart kissed her, she knew this was where she was meant to be.

He came over her, stiff muscles pressing her into the covers. His fingers glowed as he drew them along her breasts. Magick clung to her, tingling. Her thighs parted, welcoming him between them. His thick arousal pressed against her hip, spreading his tingling magick like his fingers. The pleasure of his touch intensified. Blue lights danced between them, swirling around as if to create a cocoon of pure gratification.

She arched into him, moaning his name softly, "Raibeart."

He kissed her chest and neck, each pass of his lips growing more desperate. She gripped his ass, urging him inside of her.

Raibeart would not be deterred from his mission as he kissed the length of her body. He worked his way down to her toes before returning the journey upward. His mouth encircled her breast, giving it slow attention before moving on to the other. Fingers grazed her inner thigh. Magick frolicked wherever he touched her, helping to stir her desires.

His lips grazed down her stomach, teasing

flesh with the tip of his tongue. Katherine focused on where he would make contact next. She gripped his shoulders, pushed his head, and pulled on his hair. Her hips arched in offering, and his head dipped toward her sex. Raibeart nipped at the sensitive skin where her thigh met her pussy. She moaned at the intense pleasure. He kissed her deeply, intimately pressing his tongue between her folds.

Time held no meaning, only desire.

The energy of his magick pulsed and brightened. It vibrated over her entire frame and glimmered on his skin. The air picked up around them. Leaves blew across their bodies.

Katherine grabbed his hair and pulled him upward. She needed to feel him deep. Their eyes locked as if testing to see if the moment was real.

Their bodies glowed, and tiny strands of light threaded between them whenever they parted. When they finally joined, he entered her slowly. She felt his power on her skin, inside her body. The wind picked up, causing the leaves to crash around them.

How could she have forgotten this? Him?

Katherine became determined to remember everything, never to forget his face or touch. They were bonded. Nothing would ever tear them apart again.

Raibeart belonged to her. She was his. This was everything.

She wanted the moment to last forever, but their bodies had other plans. Within a few strokes, she began to tremble, jerking as her climax ripped through her. His magick exploded around them into sparkling stars that fell to the earth before disappearing.

Katherine gasped for breath. Her heart hammered so loud she could hear it drumming in her ears. "I don't remember it being like that before."

"It would seem time has taught my magick a few tricks," he answered with a self-satisfied grin.

"I feel like I should have a clever answer for that, but my brain is mush, and I just want to rest here." She laughed softly, weakly reaching to pat his shoulder before letting her hand drop to the ground.

Raibeart settled next to her. Staying close, they both stared up at the night sky. His hip and thigh pressed alongside hers. She dropped her arm against him, letting her hand land on his chest. She felt his deep breaths punctuated by the fast beat of his heart.

"Ya rest, love." He waved his hand, drawing their kilts over them like a blanket as he wrapped his fingers around her wrist and held her hand against him. "I promise to protect ya."

It felt as if everything had been building to this moment. They were meant to be here together. Alice had tried to pry them apart, but love didn't listen to commands. A curse might make them forget, but it couldn't kill something so beautiful. It took their physical bodies coming together to make them remember the details their hearts had always known.

"Please let this be real," Katherine fought the urge to sleep. "Don't let me wake back up in the cottage."

"Aye, love, this is real."

Chapter Twelve

Raibeart felt mist prickling his legs, and his eyes opened at the warning. He reached for Katherine, but she had disappeared, and he was no longer in the forest.

He had just promised to protect her. Why had his mind brought him back here? In this dream? He wasn't supposed to be here. The nightmares were supposed to be over. They had found each other again. The curse had ended.

Hadn't it?

Raibeart surged to his feet, still naked, as he studied his barren surroundings. In the distance, he heard ocean waves crashing against shores and cliffs.

He felt more lucid than he had in a very long time. Dreams were usually impressions, feelings, their landscape changing like the rippling on a pond's surface. Rocks would shimmer and disappear, giving the impression of travel even when he didn't move his feet.

Raibeart recognized this place. He'd been here with Alice and then Gregory. His nightmare world was Katherine's prison. He'd been searching for his lost love within its misty cage without always knowing it. And, at the end of that desperate journey, he would find her in time to see her die in horrible ways. This was the nightmare he avoided with his midnight runs and drunken stupors. This was the place where his sanity had slipped.

"She's not here." Alice's voice whispered to torment him as she always had. "But that doesn't matter. You can't have her. Not really. Not forever."

"I love her," Raibeart stated. "Centuries have not changed that. I've been looking for her."

"You have been looking for a wife, any wife." Alice laughed. "Being rejected over and over and over. How does it feel? How does it feel to know you are not wanted?"

"I will never love ya, Alice," Raibeart refused to move. It wouldn't matter which direction he ran, at the end would be a death echo of Katherine taking her life.

"What happened to you?" Alice appeared before him, her face made of fog. "Why aren't you running to find her? She needs you to save her, Raibeart."

"This is how ya have been doing it, isn't it? Ya bring me here to feed off my power while I'm distracted inside your game. But I'm not playing it anymore. Katherine is not here. She's with me in the real world and you can't force her to go with ya. My family will make sure of it."

Alice smiled. A hand appeared from the mist to touch his face. He recoiled, turning his check away from her.

"Searching isn't the only game we play in here," Alice said.

The rocks began to tremble as the ground cracked open. Raibeart refused to run, even as a fissure came dangerously close to his foot. He had no magick here, just his will to stand up to the evil seductress.

Broken cottage walls grew like teeth of stone from the earth, the exterior slamming together with loud thuds as pebbles trickled to the ground. The roof blew from a growing hill as the landscape transformed. Inside the murky windows, he felt a stirring of dark magick. A path gathered outside its door leading to his feet.

"I'm not going to the window to watch," he denied, knowing what he had seen last time.

Alice's face blew away in the mist as the bleating of a goat sounded in the distance. The lights flickered inside, illuminating the darkness outside. He watched Alice swirl, only to emerge in a more solid form as the cottage door opened. The blurry image of her walked from the door around the side of the cottage to where the silhouette of a goat appeared in growing moonlight.

The woman began to chant, the faint sound vaguely familiar in a way all pacts with some devil sounded familiar. Time skipped like a film projector roll missing pieces of the story. In one instance, her hand was in the air wielding a knife. In the next, the goat lay on the ground, silent, and she carried a goblet back to the house. When the door opened, he heard his voice singing a drunken war ballad. The moment was brief as the door slammed shut.

Raibeart frowned, drawn to peek inside even though he had told himself he wouldn't. He crept toward the window, automatically trying not to be detected by the ghostly images he spied on.

He saw himself sitting at a table before a fire. Empty bottles littered the ground around him. Another soldier had passed out on the floor, curled into a ball.

Alice swiped his goblet and replaced it with her bloody one. He'd been too drunk to notice. Her lips moved, and though he couldn't hear what she said, he knew she was beckoning him to drink, promising that it would end the pain inside him.

Raibeart slammed his hand against the glass to stop the play, cracking it. Alice glanced up at him, and the glass instantly mended itself.

Raibeart watched himself drink the potion. Time skipped forward, and he was standing up from the table. It skipped several more times to show Alice holding his hand, leading him back to her bedroom.

"That treacherous witch slipped me a magickal mickey," Raibeart muttered. He had not gone with her willingly.

Not that any of that mattered now, not really. The damage was done.

Alice suddenly appeared before him in the window, grinning. Her lips stretched too wide across her face. The look startled him, and he stepped back. She was doing it again, feeding on him.

A faint scream caught his attention. Alice's smile instantly fell as she began to screech in protest.

Raibeart ignored her as he turned, darting away from the cottage. The trees of the

MacGregor forest appeared around him, and he charged toward Katherine's cry.

"What devil's spawn are ya?" Katherine demanded. She stood naked, hands raised in fists like she was about to fight a ghost.

"Katherine?" He started toward her.

A familiar chattering caught his attention, and he stopped. The veiled gremian jumped up from the ground only to land in the same spot with a pout. It chattered angrily, pointing at the lovers' forest bed. She waved her hands over her head before punching her gnarled fist into the air at Katherine.

"Easy," Raibeart tried to soothe the creature.

Katherine backed up in confusion. The gremian's friends came from the forest, some hanging from tree branches and others cautiously inching forward as they watched what transpired.

The gremian's eyes whipped toward him. She jerked the tattered veil off her head and continued to chatter aggressively as she threw it at him. The light material fluttered in the air a foot away from her. She jumped on top of it to force it to the ground faster and twisted her feet against the lace to grind it into the dirt. She repeatedly pointed at Katherine in her rage.

"Och, no, don't be upset about—"

The gremian swept her hand to shut him up

before leaping into the forest. The others followed her. He heard branches cracking under their weights as they swung quickly away.

"What was that thing?" Katherine asked, slightly breathless. Her fists were slower to drop.

"Gremian," Raibeart answered. "Poor thing is upset."

Katherine went to the discarded lace and picked it up. She held it before him. "She acted almost...*hurt*."

"She thought we'd be married," Raibeart answered.

"I know everyone keeps saying ya ask everyone to marry ya, but...." Katherine held the lace out to him. "Really?"

"No." He took the lace veil and tossed it aside. They were both naked, and he was drawn to go to her again. "I may be eccentric, but I didn't ask the question she apparently heard."

"I see." Her eyes lowered, and she looked at her feet. "Where did ya go?"

"The cottage in the mist." He wrapped his arms around her, pulling her against his chest. "I saw Alice. It was her place before it was your prison. I saw what happened the night I was with her. She used a potion to seduce me. She brings me there in my dreams to torture me so that she can keep hold of my magick."

"She doesn't love ya," Katherine said. "Sometimes people believe things for so long they can't see any other truth. I thought death was the only way I could leave the cottage, but I was wrong. Alice is wrong too. She is confusing love and possession. She wants to control ya."

"Aye." He agreed. "And she's not going to be pleased when she realizes she can't tap into my magick anymore. Now that I know how she's getting in, I'll find a way to stop her."

Leaves crunched, and they both turned to see who had intruded.

Donovan appeared within the clearing before promptly turning around. "Oh, for the love of... no child should have to see his parents naked."

Katherine scooped the earasaid from the ground and wrapped it around her body. Raibeart was slower to grab his kilt.

"Are ya sure you're my son?" Raibeart asked. "I don't think any fruit of my loins would—"

Katherine hit him lightly on the chest.

"Ya remember?" Donovan asked, surprised.

Raibeart nodded. "Aye. Things haven't been jumping out of my head as of late."

"I'm sorry, I don't remember being pregnant or giving birth," Katherine said. "I'm sure it was possible, but...."

"She took us before we were born." Gregory appeared next to his twin.

Katherine tilted her head. "I remember seeing ya as young boys, briefly, just long enough to know what was taken away. Then it was just my parents and my brothers, though I watched for ya. I'm sorry the memories faded. I'm sorry I couldn't hold on to them."

"Ya weren't meant to hold on to them. The fact that they're coming back at all is a miracle," Donovan answered.

"Ya look better than last I saw ya, Ma," Gregory said.

"Alice left the portal open sometimes, and we used to follow her in," Donovan explained. "On the nights ya decided to kill yourself, she'd get particularly excited and wouldn't…."

Katherine lifted her hand to stop him. She crossed over to their sons and lightly touched each on the cheek. "Ya look like your grandfather and uncles."

"We lived with them for a time, your parents," Gregory said.

"Alice told them ya died in shame for having us out of wedlock," Donovan added.

Raibeart felt more than saw Katherine's pain at the admission.

"I should have liked to have been there for

ya," Katherine said, "but I'm happy ya were able to know them. I know they would have loved ya deeply when I wasn't able to."

"What are ya laddies doing out here?" Raibeart asked. "Is there more trouble?"

"No, ah…" Gregory looked at Donovan. "We wondered if we might…."

"Get an invitation into the house while the family can see us," Donovan finished. He appeared to be the blunter of the two brothers. "Euann renewed the protection spells. We're not exactly on the guest list."

"Aye, go in," Raibeart waved a hand in dismissal. "Ya are MacGregors."

"Actually, we're not," Gregory said. "Alice gave us her family surname. English."

Raibeart choked in surprise and coughed as he pounded his chest. "Gregory and Donovan English?"

"Aye," the twins stated in unison.

"No sons of mine," Raibeart refuted. "I dub thee MacGregor. None of this English nonsense. Never mention it to your uncles. I'll never hear the end of it."

"Raibeart, they are old enough to decide their own names," Katherine said as she pulled on her boots. "Besides, maybe they wish to be Galbraith after my family."

"Fine," Raibeart agreed. "Galbraith-MacGregor. Very modern of us."

"Ya can't decide our name," Gregory stated.

"Aye. We're your parents. We can name ya Petey Pumpkin if we want." Raibeart pointed at the covers on the ground. "Pick that up for your ma, Donovan, and carry it back to the mansion. Come, Petey, my boy. Time to meet your relatives."

"Ya can't name me Petey," Gregory protested.

Katherine covered her smile as she walked into the forest, trying not to laugh.

"No backtalk," Raibeart stated. "You're not too old to ground."

"Aye, I am," Gregory insisted. "Donovan. Help me out here."

Donovan carried the covers under his arm and moved to follow Katherine. "Sorry, Pete. I can't help ya. It looks like I'm ma and da's favorite."

Chapter Thirteen

Waking from the dreamless black of sleep was nothing new. The shock was finding herself anywhere but inside the cottage when her eyes opened. Three days had passed, and yet each morning, she expected the cold gaze of Alice to be staring down at her from a portrait. Instead, it was the dark wood of the MacGregor guest room.

Raibeart barely left her side, and in the mornings, she found him awake and staring at her. He didn't say it, but she knew he worried she would disappear. She couldn't blame him. She had the same fear. Her eyes constantly went to the floor to watch for curling mist.

The more they connected physically, and the more exposure she had to his magick, the better she felt. They made love often. Her hands couldn't stay off him. Her mouth ached to kiss him. Her body gravitated in his direction. Whereas at first it hurt to touch him, now it hurts to be away. Raibeart was her sanity and her salvation, and she was his.

"He's sharper when he's by your side," Cait said, placing a coffee mug in front of Katherine on the dining room table. She nodded to where Raibeart had disappeared into the kitchen to emphasize her meaning.

The woman insisted everyone drink the potion in the morning. Who was Katherine to question the magick? Alice had not returned since Raibeart saw her in the forest, so whatever they were doing must have been working.

"It's not just him. I feel better when Raibeart is nearby, stronger," Katherine admitted. When he walked into another room, the names of certain items slipped her mind—like what they called this magickal drink. Only when he returned did the words come back.

"That dress looks good on ya," Cait continued. She'd insisted on updating Katherine's wardrobe to help her acclimate to modern life. The ankle-length skirt flared from the waist, and the long sleeve shirt pulled tight against the bodice. The two-piece outfit was lighter than she was used to, but at least it covered as a dress should. She had seen a woman wearing shorts that didn't completely cover the bottom of her ass, and no one but a few men appeared to notice it. Katherine wasn't sure she'd be secure enough to wear such a thing.

"Thank ya for accommodating me with it," she said.

Cait sat next to her and turned in her seat to stare. "I don't remember ya. From the old days. Margareta doesn't remember ya either."

"I never met his family," Katherine answered, wishing the woman would look away.

"He never told us about ya," Cait continued.

The fact stung, but who knew the reasoning for such a thing all these years later? She forced herself to sip the hot drink.

"Because you're a busybody, Cait," Raibeart stated. "And maybe I didn't want to share her with your lady parties."

"Lady parties?" Cait arched a brow.

Raibeart winked at Kathrine. "Aye. When ya get together, and hen talk about your bleedings and whatnots, and pick out doily patterns and trade spells."

"That's what ya think women do when they get together?" Cait chuckled.

"I'm sure there are tea and biscuits too," he dismissed. "Speaking of doilies, I left my crocheted pants for ya to mend. They snagged on the thigh."

"Aye." Cait stood from the table. "I burned them. All fixed."

When they were alone in the dining room, Raibeart sat in Cait's chair and said, "It doesn't matter. I ordered a bee costume online with a giant stinger on the arse. I'll buzz at her for a week."

"To what purpose?" Katherine asked, confused.

"The lady who makes them uses the money to raise her grandchildren who lost their ma," he answered. "She's too proud for a handout but enjoys the work."

"No, I meant, why buzz at Cait?"

Raibeart laughed. "Everyone needs a hobby. She's easy to rile. Feel free to try it sometime. Fretting keeps her young."

He reached for Katherine's mug. "Och, what is this swill?" He sniffed it. "Hazelnut?"

Katherine lifted her hands, unsure.

"Don't drink that." Raibeart pushed it aside.

"But don't we need the magick to keep Alice away?"

Raibeart laughed. "Coffee isn't that kind of magick."

"If it's not that, then…?" Kathrine didn't try to reclaim the drink. "Why is Alice staying away?"

"I don't think she'll stay away forever." He put a hand on her leg as he leaned toward her. "Now that we know how she's been stealing my magick, we were able to close off her access. Plus, our sons are with us, not her. That doesn't mean it's over. She's probably regrouping for her next attack."

"It's heartbreaking to think we have two grown sons." Katherine touched her stomach. She never got to feel them grow or move. "Alice robbed us of their childhoods. We didn't get to raise them. I suppose it's a small favor that she didn't like babies and gave them to my parents for a few years. I feel guilty that my biggest connection is that their faces remind me of my father."

"My sweet love, ya have nothing to feel guilty about. We have them now and will show them all the love we can. They were stolen from us." His hand moved from her leg to cup her cheek. "Our lives were stolen."

She nodded.

"Even if Alice is foolish enough to come here, remember, she can't force ya to leave with her," Raibeart reminded her, not for the first time. "The magick protecting us won't let her."

Katherine again nodded that she understood.

"We are not going to let Alice steal anything

else." Raibeart kissed her softly and pressed his forehead against hers. "Not one more second."

She nodded again, not taking her gaze from his.

Katherine opened her mouth to speak, but no sound came out. Coldness crept into her toes and traveled up her legs. At first, she ignored it, but when Raibeart didn't blink or move, she slowly pulled away.

Raibeart sat frozen. His handsome face stared dreamily at where she had been moments before.

Katherine touched his face and tried to move it. "Raibeart?"

He didn't budge.

She stood. Mist covered the floor, obscuring the view of her feet. It stirred as she rushed through it.

"Cait!" Katherine hurried to the kitchen door. "Cait, I need—"

Cait stood immobile near the entryway. The woman's head was turned as if she'd eaves-dropped. Mist covered the kitchen floor and what Katherine could see of the rest of the house through the doorways. Murdoch had been walking toward them when he'd froze mid-stride.

Katherine pushed the woman's shoulder. Cait didn't move.

"Anyone?" Katherine yelled. "MacGregors?"

No one answered. She ran through the dining room, dragging her hand over Raibeart as she passed him. Entering the foyer, she called, "Gregory? Donovan? Anyone? Hello!"

A gust of mist rolled down the stairs toward her. It moved like a living thing, evil and unstoppable.

A tear rolled down her cheek. What did she do? How did she save them? She wasn't magickal. She couldn't stop whatever this was.

"Hello?" Her voice cracked with fear.

Part of her wanted to hide underneath the table and bury her head in Raibeart's lap until the threat went away.

The world did not work like that.

A moment ago, she was happy. She was staring into her lover's eyes. She'd felt safe.

It was all too fragile.

"She can't force me to leave," Katherine whispered. "The magick will protect me."

Katherine took a deep breath to calm herself. "Alice?"

"So many pretty things." Alice appeared at the top of the stairs, dressed as she had been in the painting. She walked through the mist, stirring it around her as she slowly descended. "They say times have changed, but I think it's new fabric on an old pattern. A mansion lording over the town below. Rich and powerful warlocks thinking they are above the rest of us. The feudal system has a new name, but the players have not changed."

Katherine kept a close watch on the woman. She debated between running into the dining room to protect Raibeart and running out of the front door in hopes Alice would follow her and get away from the MacGregor family.

Blue magick trailed behind Alice as she drew her hand over the banister. It wound around the wood like snakes, offshoots trailing down balusters to disappear into the mist.

"What do ya want?" Katherine asked. "I did not deserve what ya did."

"Oh, sweetling." Alice's voice had a bit of mocking to it. "Haven't you realized it yet? You are insignificant in the scheme of everything. A peasant. A pawn. You would have been dead now if not for me. I brought you forward and made you special."

Katherine could see that the woman believed what she was saying.

Alice made it to the bottom of the stairs and strode toward the dining room.

Katherine tried to step into the woman's path. "What do ya want?"

Alice waved her hand. Magick shot from her fingers and slammed into Katherine's chest.

Pain erupted as the air was knocked from her lungs. Katherine slid on the marble floor, only stopping as her back crashed against a wall. She stumbled to maintain her footing as she tried not to fall over.

Alice walked through the dining room door. Katherine pushed away from the wall to go after her. When she again saw her, Alice sat on the table next to Raibeart. Her feet swung to and fro. She held a fork from one of the place settings and scraped the tines along his neck.

"Did he really think he could stop me from using his power?" Alice laughed. "I've been stock-piling his magick for centuries. All I needed was an opening to get back in."

"What opening?" Katherine held out her hand and inched forward. She stared at the fork, wondering if she was fast enough to wrestle it away.

"More of a slip than an opening," Alice corrected.

"What slip?" Katherine's fingers flexed. *One, two...*

"*Tsk.*" Alice arched a brow in warning, stopping her attack before it started.

Katherine waited for another opening.

"We are not going to let Alice steal anything

else," Alice repeated the words Raibeart had said. "Not one more second."

Katherine frowned and crept closer when Alice's attention turned to Raibeart.

"Words have great power. He said them and opened the door enough to let me slip inside." Alice waved the fork. "So I stopped time to steal less than a second, a sliver of a moment."

"So this is your plan? Trap me here in stopped time?" Katherine forced a laugh. "Now what?"

"Well. He did say I could steal less than a second." Alice drew the fork between Raibeart's eyes and down his nose. She placed the fork down with a hard thud before picking up a spoon. She held the handle and pressed the bowl to his cheek, lightly twisting it back and forth. "I wonder how handsome he'd be without his eyes?"

"No, stop!" Katherine closed the distance and tried to snatch the silverware.

Alice's magick shot out and sent Katherine flying. She traveled a shorter distance than the last time before hitting the wall.

"I can't say I've ever seen an eyeless warlock. I wonder if they'd grow back," Alice mused. "There has to be a spell or potion for that."

"What do ya want?" Katherine asked.

"He said I couldn't steal another second."

Alice ran her finger over his mouth. "But he never said you couldn't give it to me willingly."

"Ya want a second?" Katherine didn't understand.

Alice grinned.

Katherine's heart raced. "Ya want longer?"

Alice's grin widened. She tapped the spoon against Raibeart's forehead.

Katherine took a deep breath. "Ya want eternity."

Alice nodded. "And you're going to give it to me. Freely."

"Ya can't force me to go with ya. I won't." Katherine shook her head in denial. She couldn't willingly walk back into her prison, knowing what hundreds of years felt like. Only this time, Alice wasn't asking for a hundred years or even five hundred. She wanted forever.

"Give me what I want or…" Alice placed the spoon back on the table and grabbed the fork.

"Ya won't—"

Alice stabbed the fork into Raibeart's neck. Katherine gasped and tried to stop her. Alice again shoved her away with magick.

This time Katherine's head hit the wall, and her vision blurred. When she could again focus, she saw the fork in Raibeart's neck. He hadn't moved, and the wound didn't bleed.

"If ya kill him ya lose your magick," Katherine reasoned.

"It might not kill him, but I can make him hurt." Alice held the spoon against the inner corner of his eye. "First, I'll take Raibeart's eyes, and then I'll kill his family, and then I'll behead your traitorous sons. All in this tiny little sliver of a moment."

"Aye. I'll go." Katherine didn't push away from the wall. "Just promise ya won't hurt him, *any* of them."

Alice considered the words for a moment before slamming the spoon down on the table and leaping to her feet. "Nice try, but the whole point of taking you away from him is to hurt him. However, if you go, I promise not to hurt them in this less-than-a-second. After that, you will be gone, and I won't need to resort to such primitive torture methods."

What choice did she have?

Katherine nodded. "Where?"

"To your room." Alice tilted her head toward Raibeart's bedroom.

Katherine looked at Raibeart. The fork remained in his neck. When she lifted her hand to pull it out, Alice *tsked* at her.

Katherine left the fork alone. She had to trust that his magick would save him when time resumed.

"Time to go," Alice stated, her tone losing any semblance of patience.

Raibeart's eyes were thankfully intact and still gazing lovingly to where she had been sitting. She would remember that expression forever. She would have to.

Katherine trembled as she tried to make her legs move. She didn't want to leave him, didn't want to step back into her cage. Before, there had always been the hope that someday she'd find a way out. But now, she'd go back in, knowing there was more waiting for her and unable to return.

"I love ya," she told Raibeart. He couldn't hear it, but she needed to say it. "These days with ya have been—"

Magick hit her in the stomach, doubling her over. Pain radiated throughout her entire body. It vibrated her bones and made her skin feel like she'd been set on fire. Katherine fell onto the dining room floor. She braced herself on her hands and tried to draw a breath.

"You are so tedious." Alice kicked Katherine's elbow, knocking her support.

Katherine fell into the mist. Before she could push herself up, Alice grabbed her hair and pulled her across the floor.

"Stop!" Katherine kicked, trying to stop the momentum. "I'll walk."

Katherine's knee slammed into the doorway, and she cried out in pain. She scrambled to grab hold of Cait's frozen ankle. Her body jerked, and Alice dropped her hair.

"I'll walk," Katherine repeated. She managed to stand.

Cait hadn't moved.

Alice let the magick dance along her fingers.

Katherine stepped past her, carefully facing the woman as she moved through the kitchen. Not turning her back fully, she walked sideways into the hallway. Murdoch blocked her path, and she had to weave past him.

Alice paused next to Murdoch and looked at him in contemplation.

"Hey, we had a deal," Katherine warned. "Ya can't hurt them."

Alice wrinkled her nose in irritation but left Murdoch alone.

Katherine stopped outside Raibeart's room. She had to hope that Alice would honor their deal once she was imprisoned.

"Open it," Alice ordered.

Katherine hesitated. Though she fought them, tears trailed down her face. She shook her head.

"I don't want to do this. Please, Alice, enough. Ya don't—"

Alice waved her hand, opening the door.

Katherine stared at the familiar chamber. She looked at Alice, but the woman had no sympathy.

Katherine touched the doorframe and looked at the fireplace. Raibeart's portrait stared back at her. She gazed up at his handsome face and held onto the feeling of love she carried. She stepped inside.

The door slammed behind her.

Katherine took a deep breath, still looking at the picture. "My name is Katherine Galbraith. This is not my home. I am a prisoner of bad magick. I have two sons, Gregory and Donovan. My name is Katherine, and I am in love with Raibeart MacGregor. My name is Katherine Galbraith. This is not my home...."

Chapter Fourteen

Raibeart gazed into Katherine's lovely eyes, never wanting to look away. With her, he felt whole.

Suddenly, a sharp sting hit his neck, and he jerked in surprise.

"Och!" He swatted at the pain, and a fork flew to the ground. "What devilry is...? Katherine?"

Katherine had disappeared from her chair. He held his bleeding neck as he leaned to look under the table. She wasn't hiding there.

"Katherine!" he yelled. "Where did ya go, love?"

Cait limped into the room from the kitchen. She leaned to the side, favoring her left ankle.

"Is she in there?" Raibeart demanded.

Cait shook her head in denial as she reached down to rub her leg. "She was in here. With ya."

"My Cait?" Murdoch went to his wife and kneeled next to her to look at her foot. "What happened? What is it?"

"I don't know. It just started hurting," Cait said.

"Did ya see Katherine?" Raibeart asked Murdoch.

His brother shook his head in denial even as he examined his wife. "Is this bruise a handprint? Did someone do this to ya?"

"Raibeart, what's wrong with your neck?" Cait demanded. "Why are ya bleeding?"

"Katherine!" Raibeart sprinted to the foyer, ignoring Cait's concern. He went halfway up the stairs. "Katherine!"

Donovan and Gregory came onto the landing from where they had been staying in guest rooms.

"What's happened?" Gregory asked.

"Dono. Petey." Raibeart waved his hand frantically. "Your ma is missing. Did she come up there?"

The boys shook their heads.

"We haven't seen her," Donovan said.

Gregory frowned and lifted his hand as if to sense something in the air. "I think Alice was here."

Raibeart switched directions. He took the steps two at a time until he made a giant leap onto the foyer's marble floor. He landed, running for the front door. Using his magick, he flung it open.

"Katherine! Katherine!"

He yelled for her, trying to sense her nearness, but his magick came up empty. Alice shouldn't have been able to force her to leave. The protection spells were still in place.

"Show yourself," he ordered, looking for signs of life in the surroundings. Tiny blue lights revealed the location of bunnies next to the garage. More lights erupted from over the town to show the locals. None of that helped him.

"Katherine!"

Raibeart spun in circles, not knowing where to go.

"Raibeart, come inside," Cait called from the door. She braced her hand against the frame while using Murdoch for counter support. "We'll figure this out."

"She was right there. I was looking at her and then...gone." Raibeart didn't know what to do or where to go. He lifted his hand before his face. "She was right there."

Raibeart felt his clarity slipping. Fear rolled through him. He knew the familiar emptiness creeping into his soul.

"How did Alice get in?" he asked Cait,

growing desperation filling each moment. "We blocked her from taking my magick."

"We blocked her from taking *more* of your magick," Cait corrected. "Who knows what other resources she has? But Alice should not have gotten into the mansion, and she should not have been able to take Katherine out. Katherine must be inside somewhere."

"We'll find her," Murdoch tried to reassure him. "Alice won't get away with this."

Raibeart ran inside to search the house. What else could he do? He'd been looking for Katherine for centuries, searching and searching even as he'd forgotten what he had looked for. He asked countless women to marry him, hoping to stir just the memory of what he felt like with Katherine. He'd known a piece was missing, and that had been his clumsy attempt to find it.

"She was right in front of me," he told himself, willing her to reappear. How could he have lost her when he was looking right at her? How did he fight his own magick being used against him?

"Katherine!"

Desperation filled Raibeart until reason held no meaning. There was only the searching need, worse than before, because it had a name. Her name.

"Katherine!"

He ran from room to room, using his magick to fling open every door. Cabinets slammed and clanged as if she'd be hiding amongst the pots and pans or crammed into a narrow shelf next to a bag of flour. Desk drawers flew from their safe little homes, sprinkling pens and letter openers like hard confetti. Papers fluttered into the mess.

"Katherine!"

Bedroom doors flung wildly open, revealing empty secrets within their clean interiors. Murdoch and Cait's looked like a catalog from a 1950s magazine. Angus and Margareta slept in shabby chic comfort. Fergus and Donna's appeared like a bedroom template waiting to be designed because they were never home. His magick disheveled all of them, overturning the beds and emptying the dressers.

Raibeart stopped outside his bedroom door. His magick hit the wood and bounced back over him, not opening. He reached for the knob, twisting it violently so it rattled against the lock.

"Katherine!"

He pounded on the wood and slammed his shoulder into it. She hated that room. She would never have gone in there willingly.

"Katherine? Love?"

He pressed his ear to the door, listening anxiously for a sign that she was there.

"Raibeart..." His name whispered from within, so soft it might have been his hopeful imagination tormenting him.

He sank to his knees, hitting it with his fist and head, shaking the knob to let him in. He tried to look through the keyhole but it was black on the other side. His magick blasted against the barrier, sapping his strength, only to bounce back at him.

"Please, Katherine, I can't lose ya. Not again. Please, Katherine, come back...."

Chapter Fifteen

Katherine stood before her old friend the cursed hallway mirror and watched helplessly as Raibeart tried to reach her. Blood streamed down his neck, but he was alive. In that, she took small comfort.

She glanced down the hall of the cottage to the bedroom, to the twin of the door he now knocked on. Their hallways were very different, but that room remained a reflection of both their worlds.

Katherine had no memories of them together in that room beyond her first escape. They had avoided it while at the MacGregor mansion. But she didn't need a bed to remember the feel of him on her skin or the taste of his kiss.

Her greatest fear was that those memories would fade as months turned into years to decades and centuries. She had lost him before. How long had she been able to cling to him until the portrait in the bedroom staring down at her had become just another object inside her prison walls? How long until she forgot to repeat his name or mispronounced it?

Here time was the ultimate enemy.

Katherine stared into the mirror. Hopefully, the image would remain, and she could watch him like this, and in a way, it would be like she was with him.

"Raibeart," she whispered as he pressed his ear to the door. "Raibeart. Your name is Raibeart MacGregor, and I am in love with ya. She can't have that."

"I love to watch you scurry around like a little mouse in a trap." Alice appeared next to her.

Katherine jumped back from the mirror to face the woman.

"You're my favorite pet." Alice reached to tuck a strand of hair behind Katherine's ear.

Katherine jerked away. The resistance only seemed to amuse Alice.

"My name is Katherine," Alice mocked. "My parents are dead, and I cannot die."

"Why can't ya just end this?" Katherine knew begging was pointless, but what else could she do?

"Oh, I could." Alice laughed, the sound giving

away the fact that she had no intention of doing so. "I was starting to grow bored with this game. Watching you wallow and wander and wallow and wander. Counting all the thousands of ways you endeavored to die. This game of ours needs to be refreshed, don't you think?"

Katherine shook her head in denial. That did not sound like a fun idea.

"Good. You agree." Alice grinned.

Alice sauntered more than walked as she made her way toward the front of the cottage. Her shoes thumped on the hard floors. Katherine was slow to follow. She glanced at Raibeart in the mirror as she took a small step. He was still desperate to get inside the room.

"Enough of that," Alice stated.

The mirror disappeared. Katherine gasped, reaching toward the discolored paint on the wall where it had hung.

"Now, let's see," Alice's loud voice drifted as she went around the corner. "What should we change? New home?"

Katherine had no choice but to follow and watch.

"No. There's comfort in the familiar, isn't there?" Alice laughed. "But I did like the MacGregor's dining room. Perhaps we can…"

The table shimmered and changed. The

cottage wall grew longer to accommodate a long table with more chairs than Katherine would ever need in her isolation. It was a perfect replica of the MacGregor table. The two chairs where she had sat with Raibeart were pulled away from the table and turned slightly toward each other.

"What do you think?" Alice asked.

Katherine found herself going toward the chair. She touched the back of Raibeart's seat and couldn't stop her hands from shaking. The smell of hazelnut coffee scented the air. He had called it swill. The spoon and fork place setting reminded her of why she had returned to this hell.

"It's almost like you can feel him, but not quite. If you get there fast enough each morning, maybe the seat will be warm with his heat." Alice laughed.

"How did ya become so heartless?" Katherine whispered. A tear slipped down her face. She couldn't feel his heat in the chair's back, and she doubted she ever would.

Still, she knew she would try.

"I agree. Much better." Alice nodded, tapping the corner of her chin as she looked around. "What else?"

Rain began to fall. Lightning streaked across the sky, illuminating the windows. It pelted the roof as the sound of a heavy wind whistled its way through the window frames. Thunder boomed loudly in the heavens as if threatening any who dared to venture outside.

"Change of décor. Change of atmosphere." Alice pretended to think. "Change of appetite."

A feast appeared on the table. Some of the foods she'd seen from Cait's many offerings— donuts and pastries. Many she could no longer name since she wasn't under the comfort of Raibeart's nearness.

"But this is not the worst part for you, is it?" Alice studied Katherine. "It's the loneliness, isn't it? Pacing around, talking to yourself, answering yourself."

Katherine was too afraid to answer. There was a cruelness in Alice's gaze, a determined nastiness that just waited for opportunities to dig its evil, bitchy claws into its prey.

"Change of company." Alice smiled.

Katherine looked around, listening for a sign of whom Alice had brought to stay in the prison with her.

"Well then. I'll leave you to get acquainted." Alice waved her fingers and strode to the front door. As she opened it, a bright flash of lightning consumed her, and she disappeared.

"Alice?" Katherine asked, running to shut the

door as the angry rainfall slanted in. She pushed it closed, latching it so it wouldn't blow open.

The fireplace flickered, the light from the flames dimming. Outside, the storm gave flashes of light but otherwise contributed very little. A chair moved, scraping against the floor. She jumped back, staring at the empty space.

"Hello?" she called weakly. "Raibeart, is that ya?"

It was too much to hope for, and she knew Alice would never have let him come here.

Unsettling noises came from the hallway. She recognized them from the forest. What had Raibeart called the creatures?

Katherine looked around for a weapon and only saw the fork. She ran to snatch it off the table. The sound of feet pattered around her at the decision. She turned, wielding the pathetic weapon.

The shadows seemed to move but were too dark to reveal whatever surprises hid inside. Katherine remembered the anger in the discarded bride, her sharpened teeth and miniature claws. Chattering came from all over the cottage as if the creatures spoke to each other.

"My name is Katherine," she said, trying to be brave. Alice had said they were company. Perhaps if she treated them as such, they wouldn't hurt her. "Welcome to my home."

A plate rattled, and she saw one of them near the pile of donuts munching away. He chattered loudly to the others, and more emerged to attack the table. Silverware clanged on the floor, and plates broke as they made a mess of their feasting.

Katherine couldn't go outside into the raging storm. There was only one option. She kept an eye on the guests as she moved toward the hall to escape. A few of them glanced at her but were thankfully too engrossed in their meal to bother coming after her.

When she was out of sight, Katherine ran toward the bedroom. She slammed the door shut behind her and crossed over to the bed. Looking to see the comfort of Raibeart's face gazing down at her, she was met with a different portrait. Her love was gone, leaving only the image of Alice standing in front of the MacGregor mansion. The evilness of her cold eyes and half smile was worse than before. She had taken away the mirror and the image, the two visuals that would have connected her memories to Raibeart.

A loud chatter came from the bed. Katherine spun to face it, wielding her pathetic fork.

The discarded bride clutched the tattered veil in her hand. The creature leaped, claws and fangs extended. Katherine tried to defend herself, but the fork bent instead of piercing the creature's hard skin.

Fingers clawed her face as teeth sunk into her neck. Katherine screamed in pain. She tried to throw the creature off, squirming around and bumping into furniture and walls in her haste. Her energy soon failed her, and she fell to the hard floor. The creature released her, ranting wildly. She heard the door open but couldn't move to see it. The sound of footsteps ran from the room.

In her pain, bleeding out, her eye locked onto the portrait over the fireplace, to where Alice stared down smiling. Katherine understood that this was the new game. Alice would make her long for loneliness by tormenting her. When the pain stopped, Katherine would wake up in bed ready to do it all over again.

This was Alice's new nightmare.

Chapter Sixteen

Raibeart watched the mirror in horror as the gremian attacked Katherine. She was defenseless against the angry creature.

"Where did that come from?" Cait asked, indicating the mirror that hung outside Raibeart's locked bedroom door. "Is that Katherine? Is she…?"

Cait moved to push open Raibeart's bedroom door. Inside it was empty.

"It's Alice's mirror," Donovan said. He and his brother had joined them in the hallway. "Careful. It's made of dark magick."

"The mirror just appeared to show me Katherine." Raibeart touched the glass, trying to reach inside. His fingers hit the barrier. He felt the enchanted object pulling his magick out of his hand. He jerked it away, not wanting to give Alice any more of his power.

Katherine blinked one last time before lifeless eyes stared. The image disappeared, leaving his horrified reflection looking back at him.

Every sorrow that had ever been felt within the history of the world filled his heart. He tried to scream, but only a groan left his throat.

"She's not dead," Donovan assured him.

"She can't die in there," Gregory added. "It's part of the curse."

The twins sounded sad and resigned as if they had seen this show before.

Slowly the heartbreak turned to rage, burning into him, and forcing strength into his legs to keep him standing. Alice had taken so much from his family. She stole his children. She tortured his sanity. She broke his love's heart.

"Raibeart?" Cait whispered, her voice shaking. "Your hands."

His magick had gathered over his clenched fists, turning a deep red.

Thump-thump. Thump-thump.

He saw Cait talking, but he couldn't hear the words. They became lost in the hard pounding of his heart as it echoed in his ears.

Raibeart had always trusted his magick and followed it without question. Usually, he could depend upon it. He often saw and understood things that most people could not. When he saw a stranger passing in a crowd, he knew what was wrong and how to help. When Maura and Curtis were stuck in a time loop, Raibeart had seen their repeated travels. When Kenneth appeared with a child, Raibeart was the one who understood what Jewel needed, and it had nothing to do with her phoenix powers. The examples were endless. His family thought him off-kilter and silly. They said he made little sense and treated him like a child.

His magick had never failed him. Or so he thought.

Thump-thump.

For all the good his magick had done, he hadn't known it was also part of his biggest betrayal as it was filtered through Alice's ill will.

Thump-thump. Thump-thump. Thump-thump.

The red magick burned up Raibeart's arms, and the sound of his heart grew louder. Murdoch appeared to be screaming at him as he ushered his wife back. Cait took off limp-running with Murdoch right behind her.

"Da?" Gregory's lips moved to form the word, but the sound was as lost as the rest of it. "Da?"

Donovan appeared before him and gave a little shrug as he mouthed, "Sorry, Da."

Donovan lifted a fist covered in blue magick

and punched his father. Raibeart blinked in surprise as his head snapped back. Sound returned.

"…didn't want to do that," Donovan was saying.

As Raibeart slumped, Gregory and Donovan caught him under the arms. They began dragging him down the hallway.

"I'm looking forward to the day we can stop rescuing our parents," Gregory said. "Let's hope Cait's potion works to neutralize this rage."

"At least he's not naked this time," Donovan answered.

Gregory snorted. "Aye, thank the heavens for small blessings."

Chapter Seventeen

Ghosts weren't so bad.

Katherine watched a dining chair float over the ceiling as she sipped the hazelnut coffee. She hated the taste, but it reminded her of Raibeart, and she'd take any connection she could get to him. She still wore the skirt and shirt Cait had given her. Alice hadn't bothered assigning her a nightgown, so she woke up in the same dress each time.

Ethereal laughter seemed to come from inside the walls. Every once in a while, a door would open and then slam shut.

All right, ghosts were annoying, but at least they weren't gremians. It had taken a few trips through the cottage cycle, but she'd finally remembered what those first little terrors were called. Gremians.

After the gremians, she awoke to find an ill-tempered unicorn on her lawn. The rain had stopped, but the stabby beast didn't let her leave the house. Next, there were singing fairies. Their high-pitched voices held all the beauty of glass shattering inside eardrums. After that, she awoke inside a spider's web.

Alice was undoubtedly a...

What was one of those new words she'd learned during her time in reality?

Asshole. Alice was an asshole.

The chair dropped onto the floor, splintering into pieces. She jolted in surprise but didn't react otherwise.

Katherine remained in her chair, facing Raibeart's empty seat as she imagined him next to her. She finished her coffee and stared into the empty mug for a long moment. Disembodied footsteps ran over the floor before her bedroom door slammed shut. She placed the mug on the table.

A giggle sounded, and the mug flew from the table and crashed against the mantel. The bedroom door slammed again, and this time the footsteps skipped.

"You can't hide," two young girls sang in

unison. "You can't seek. You can't find the will to speak."

The girls appeared from the hallway, skipping to a stop to stand in front of the table. They stared at Katherine. They wore matching ankle boots and white dresses with blue stripes. The knee-length skirts puffed out from thick petticoats. Their translucent figures were clear enough to reveal brown eyes and dark blonde ringlets falling against their cheeks. Though they appeared to be the picture of innocence, Katherine did not trust them. This was Alice's game.

The girls continued to stare as if waiting for Katherine to acknowledge them.

Katherine took a donut and watched as her fingers sunk into the soft surface to make little dents.

"We're not bound anymore. We're not leaving like before," the girls sang.

Katherine glanced up to see they had moved closer. She resumed her examination of the donut.

One of the girls crawled on top of the table. "They don't know that we're here."

The second one joined her. "But their hearts will fill with fear."

The first continued, inching closer, "They did try to send us—"

"Fine," Katherine interrupted in annoyance.

"I see ya."

The girls charged forward, their demeanors changing as their expressions darkened. Their mouths opened wide, baring little porcelain nubs of teeth in a way that would have been comical if not for their angry intent.

Cold slammed into Katherine's body as the ghosts dove through her, knocking the air from her lungs. Her vision went dark.

Katherine took a deep breath, opened her eyes, and found herself again in bed. The cold stare of Alice watched over her.

"To hell with ya, Alice," Katherine muttered.

She felt rested as if she'd slept, but she did not want to get up to see what new monster awaited her.

It was as if Alice's new goal was to keep her mind so busy that she couldn't remember Raibeart. Before, she'd been trapped in the sameness with no memories to keep her company. Now she had memories but no time in which to relive them fully.

She glared at the portrait almost defiantly and stated, "I'm in love with Raibeart MacGregor. I'm in love with Raibeart MacGregor. I'm in love with—"

A giant tentacle came from beneath the bed and slapped her across the face.

Chapter Eighteen

Raibeart carried the mirror wrapped in the red comforter from his bedroom. The padding kept it from pulling at his magick as he transported the cursed object to the back garden. Seeing Murdoch and Angus, he asked, "Did ya bring it?"

"Aye," his brothers answered in unison.

They too had a mirror wrapped in a wool blanket. Theirs was much taller and heavier, and they each carried a side.

"Margareta will not be pleased to find this missing," Angus warned. "She likes having portal access to Erik's house. Ya have to promise me ya will be careful with it."

The blanket punched up between them.

"Hey!" a muffled voice said from underneath

the wool. The material bunched together as someone from inside pulled at it.

"Set it down," Angus ordered, lowering his side to the ground. He loosened the blanket as Murdoch dropped his end.

Once the glass was free, Donovan's head appeared from within the mirror, poking up from the ground. He looked up at his uncles before reaching his arms through from the other side. He hoisted himself up, coming through the portal. Angus and Murdoch grabbed him under his arms and hauled him out of the mirror.

"We did as ya asked," Donovan said. "We told Erik there might be visitors coming through the portal. He's getting his wife out of their house."

Kneeling next to it, Donovan reached inside the mirror. His hand disappeared only to return, pulling his brother through.

"He also said this better not be like the time Malina's bad luck demon husband let trolls and goblins loose into his home through the portal," Donovan added. "Then something about Lydia's grandmother leaving her the house but also being a ghost who'd do some kind of scary threat to all of us."

Raibeart ignored the warning as he placed the cursed mirror on the ground. He didn't have time to run his entire plan by them. His family would

"What are ya doing here? Ya can't be here Raibeart. It's not safe." Katherine frowned. "I came here so ya wouldn't be harmed."

He reached for her. "I'm rescuing ya."

Katherine bounced again as she tried to hold the door. She stared down at her reflection in the mirror. "We need to block the door. I dazed a couple of them with a chair, but they recover fast."

"Trust me," he said. He stayed on the floor and pressed his back against the door to hold it for her. The creatures hit hard against it, and he heard a crack.

She nodded, still appearing unsure.

It would be a tight squeeze, but he'd make sure she made it out. After she went through the mirror, he wasn't sure what would happen. The room might reset itself without her, and he might be trapped alone.

Better him than her.

"I love ya, Katherine." Raibeart took her hand and pulled it down into the glass. Her fingers disappeared.

"Are ya sure I'm not hallucinating?"

"No, my love. The portal will take ya to Erik's house. You'll be safe there."

He had to believe his family would protect her if he didn't make it back.

"You're coming." It was a half statement, half question.

Raibeart didn't want to lie, so instead he pushed at her shoulder. "Go. Now."

Katherine fell toward the mirror as if being pulled from the other side. Her sharp cry of surprise was cut off as her head disappeared into the glass. Her body slid, and her hips became trapped by her skirt. Her feet kicked wildly in the air.

Raibeart released the door and used both hands to force her hips through the portal. The mirror's edges snagged her dress on the way through, but she disappeared inside. He watched in relief when the mirror didn't vanish on him.

A bat slammed into the door, and the wood splintered. The creature's head appeared through a hole in the wood. Several other bats kept flying into the door.

Raibeart pushed his kilt off his hips and tucked his manhood before diving toward the floor, trying to elongate his body to make it through. Someone caught his hands on the other side and jerked him forward. The mirror scraped his naked hips and thighs. Pain shot down him, but he didn't care. The cottage disappeared as he passed through the portal to enter Erik and Lydia's bedroom.

The receiving mirror was upright when he came through, and he fell toward the floor.

Gregory and Donovan panted heavily as if they had run from the gardens to this side of the portal.

"Freeze it!" Raibeart yelled.

Katherine lay on the bed, holding her neck. He crawled toward her to protect her as he leaned his body over hers.

"What?" Donovan asked.

Raibeart pointed toward the mirror just as a bangungot bat soared through. Donovan grabbed the mirror and yanked it forward, causing it to crash onto the floor. The giant creature tore around the room, knocking pictures off the walls and overturning vases.

"What in the world...?" Erik charged into his bedroom to be greeted by the commotion. He flung his hands, sending a burst of energy at the bat to petrify it. The creature instantly froze and dropped to the floor like a stone gargoyle.

Erik's rounded eyes looked at the mess they had made. The mirror had shattered in the fall. Broken vases and picture frames added to the chaos. Raibeart's blood smeared the floor. Katherine and Raibeart bled on the floral bedding.

Erik gestured at his cousins. "You two, clean

this up. My wife doesn't see the blood. She's already worried about the Alice situation." He then pointed at the bat. "Get rid of whatever the hell that thing is. I don't want it waking up outside of a cage."

"Bangungot bat," Raibeart answered. "They were extinct. Now they're apparently making a comeback."

Erik started to leave before stopping. "And for the love of everything put on clothes, Uncle Raibeart, before Lydia sees. Ya know the house rules."

"Aye," Raibeart nodded. "Could ya be a good lad, though, and send for Cait?"

Erik nodded. "Already on my way to call her. Those are nasty cuts."

Raibeart glanced at his legs, incredibly grateful the cuts were limited to his thighs and not his dangly bits.

"It's good ya got Katherine out," Erik added. "Don't worry about the portal. It's a small sacrifice."

"How did ya know that would work?" Gregory asked.

Raibeart didn't think as he admitted, "I didn't."

"We were going to come with ya, but the cursed mirror broke when ya went through,"

Donovan said. "Then we realized what ya were trying to do and ran here."

"Raibeart," Katherine whispered weakly, touching his cheek. "Don't let her put me back in there."

"No matter where ya go, I will always come for ya," he answered, refusing to close his eyes as he stared at her.

Her hand dropped as she passed out.

"Katherine?" Raibeart lightly tapped her pale cheek. The bite mark on her neck had turned red and puffy. "My love, wake up."

She didn't respond.

Raibeart cradled her in his arms. The portal mirror was broken, and suddenly the short jog to the mansion seemed too long.

"Grab the bat," Raibeart told his sons as he lifted Katherine in his arms. He rushed her through the home. "Erik, we need your car!"

Chapter Nineteen

"I thought these monstrosities were extinct." Angus stared at the bangungot bat locked in the basement cage. He'd helped Raibeart milk the creature for its venom, not exactly a welcome task for anyone involved. "From what netherworld did Alice dredge this wee one up?"

"Katherine is one lucky lady," Cait answered. "We ran out of venom centuries ago. I wouldn't have been able to make the anti-venom potion without it. She might have survived the attack, but it wouldn't have stopped her from becoming a bangungot and moving into a hollowed-out tree in the forest."

"I'm sure Raibeart wouldn't mind her sitting on his face to suffocate him," Angus answered with a chuckle.

Raibeart glanced at his brother and then gave a slight nod of agreement. That was how a bangungot killed their sleeping victims. "Aye, I can think of worse ways to go."

Joking didn't help to remove the worry banging around in his chest. He wouldn't feel at ease until Katherine opened her eyes and looked at him.

Murdoch promised not to leave her side as they retrieved the venom. Raibeart was torn between keeping her within his sight and not letting her anywhere near the bangungot bat. He also knew how dangerous milking could be and wouldn't let his brothers go near the fangs. It was bad enough that he had to ask Angus to hold the creature by the feet as it thawed from Erik's petrifying spell.

Raibeart tugged at the waist of his new kilt. The material felt too stiff and scratchy. Leaving his favorite clothing behind in Alice's cottage was a small price to pay.

"Stop fidgeting," Cait said. She, for one, was pleased to see his old kilt disappear.

"It's not the same." Raibeart frowned.

"It's exactly the same, only newer." Cait twirled a potion bottle to mix the contents inside. The brownish liquid did not look appealing. "How did ya know the portal mirror would work?"

Raibeart had been avoiding that question.

Cait stopped mixing the liquid and looked at him.

"I didn't," Raibeart answered honestly to get her to continue. "I could think of nothing else. Besides Alice, that cursed mirror was the only connection I had to reach her."

"Ya know, when ya fueled your magick to activate it, ya killed a few of Jane's favorite bushes." Cait set the bottle down and reached to pour a vial of venom into it. The milky substance was tinted with blood. "And ya destroyed Lydia's bedroom, plus ya broke the portal. We can't let anyone try to go through it now. Who knows where they'd end up?"

"I saved Katherine's life," Raibeart said, irritated that Cait felt the need to list out the damage.

"Just making conversation," she said, her lips tight as she concentrated a little too hard on the bottle. "We wish ya would have come to us for help. We like Katherine. The womenfolk aren't useless in battle. We would have helped."

"I did come to ya." He nodded at the potion bottle. "You're the only one I trust to make this, Cait."

That seemed to assuage Cait's hurt ego, and she handed the bottle to him. "Keep agitating it and pour it on the bites immediately. It loses potency fast."

Raibeart took the bottle and kept swirling it as he ran up the basement steps two at a time.

"Careful, don't spill!" Cait yelled after him. "That's all we have."

"Katherine, I'm coming!" Raibeart went to the guest bedroom where they had laid her on a bed.

Margareta had undressed Katherine and was in the process of cleaning her wounds with a washcloth. Murdoch had his back turned to give them privacy. A folded pile of clean clothes had been set near her feet.

Katherine looked as if she hadn't moved. The thin sheet covering her body revealed the entire length of her curves. Her features had taken on a gray cast as if death swirled beneath the surface. His magick surged, wanting to go to her but unable to stop whatever process had started inside her.

"I have it." Raibeart sat on the bed. His hands shook as he reached for her chin to turn her head.

"Let me." Margareta held out her hand. "She has three bites. This might sting, and I'll need ya to hold her still."

Raibeart nodded. He sat on the bed and pulled Katherine into his arms, holding her against his chest as he let her head fall against his arm to expose her neck. He brushed her hair back out of the way. Thin black lines had begun to stretch from the wound. They grew up her neck and down her chest and arm like the legs of an ugly spider. One of the legs had made it to her cheek.

Raibeart kissed the soft flesh beneath her eye and whispered, "I need ya to wake up, Katherine. Please, love, come back to me."

Margareta focused on the wound's center and held her breath as she slowly poured the anti-venom potion. Some of the potion trailed along her skin and dripped onto the bed.

"Come on. Get in there," Margareta whispered.

The liquid began to soak into the wound.

"That's a good girl," Margareta soothed.

Katherine's eyes opened wide, and she began to scream. She kicked violently to escape the pain.

Raibeart murmured to her, begging her forgiveness, professing his love, willing her to be strong and stay with him. He tightened his grip to keep her still as she fought him.

"Hold her," Margareta ordered. She lifted Katherine's arm and poured the potion on the bite she'd found near the armpit. "Murdoch, her legs."

Murdoch grabbed Katherine by the ankles to stop her kicking.

Margareta then set to work on the bite on Katherine's lower calf just above her ankle before returning to pour the remainder on the neck wound.

When Margareta finished, Murdoch let go of Katherine's ankles. The bites bubbled as if expelling the poison. The spider's legs retracted down her cheek and neck as the legs were pulled into the center wound. The screams turned to confused gasping, and Katherine lost a little of her fight.

"Raibeart?" Katherine pushed against him to see their surroundings.

"We're home, love," he assured her, not letting go. "You're safe."

Raibeart looked to Margareta for confirmation. She nodded that the potion was working.

Margareta motioned toward the stack of clothes. A loose sweatshirt and yoga pants slithered onto Katherine's body to dress her.

"Katherine, ya need to wear loose clothing only." Margareta touched her patient's head to get her attention. "Nothing tight against the bites. They need air to heal. Stay in bed. No running around. Sleep if ya can. Let the potion work."

"Aye," Katherine answered hoarsely.

Margareta waved for Murdoch to leave the room with her.

"I used to hate the boring, predictable days." Katherine closed her eyes. "I can't say the excitement of being attacked by every manner of supernatural creature is any better."

Raibeart laid her on the bed and stretched out next to her. "She shouldn't have been able to imprison ya. I don't understand how she forced you to go past the protection spells. The spells should have kept ya inside the house with me."

"She didn't force me. I went willingly. It was either that or watch her kill your entire family within a second of stopped time." Katherine sighed. "But she changed the rules of the prison. She made it worse."

"I'm sorry I didn't get there faster."

"Ya came." Katherine tried to look brave, but a tear slid down her temple as she stared at the ceiling.

"Are ya in pain?" Raibeart started to get up, intent on calling his sisters.

"No. The bites are feeling better," she said. "It's just... Maybe ya shouldn't have healed me. I don't think Alice is ever going to stop. As long as I'm alive, I'm in danger."

"Aye, we should have healed ya." He didn't like this talk from her.

"I don't want to die, but I can't live like that. Please, Raibeart, promise if a choice has to be made—"

"Shh." He put his hand to her lips, stopping her words. "Margareta placed every protection spells she knows around this room. My brothers are right outside the door. Cait is making ya a salve for later to help heal any wounds that remain after the venom is gone. Sleep easy, my love. Alice will not touch ya. I promise."

She nodded and closed her eyes.

Honestly, he wouldn't have blamed her if she didn't believe him. He felt like he'd failed her so many times before.

"Rest now. We'll talk about this later." Raibeart kissed Katherine's forehead.

The one thing he prized above all others—his love for her—was the one thing putting her in danger. She was his heart, and she needed to be protected at all costs.

As much as he wanted to, he couldn't kill Alice without killing himself. She had been tapped into his magick for too long. They were linked. There was only one other choice. Raibeart had to give Alice what she wanted.

His sweet, innocent, beautiful Katherine did not deserve this fate.

Chapter Twenty

Raibeart didn't say goodbye to Katherine. He didn't need to. She would know he had not wanted to leave her. He did not want her last memory of him to be of tears streaming down his face. He did not want his memory of her to be watching her heart shatter into pieces.

There were many things he hadn't said. Centuries' worth of things, beautiful things, funny things, sad things. Alice had stolen those conversations from them.

Raibeart would not let the evil bitch steal any more of Katherine's life.

He had thought his magick and this house would be enough to protect her. Alice had tricked her right back into a cell, one worse than before. There could not be a third time.

He did not say goodbye to his family. There was no need for words like that. They would know what he had done and why. They would be angry but would understand. They would look after Katherine like she was one of them, for she was everything to him.

He did not say goodbye to his sons. Alice had stolen the bond of fatherhood from him by taking them away until they were men. How could he explain his decision to leave them now? What could he say that would make any difference once their ma was safe? But he knew the MacGregor family would welcome them into the fold. The twins would want for nothing.

Moonlight kissed the ground, beckoning him to a midnight run. The familiar forest welcomed him like an old friend. Tonight, it all felt so lonely and did not offer an escape.

Raibeart cut across the back gardens to a forest path. He ran, keeping his clothes on. It didn't matter where he went so long as he was away from the mansion and the town.

He let his magick pull from the trees, fueling himself into a tempting treat Alice would not be able to resist. Her magick was his magick, and she'd sense him.

After a mile, he stopped and stood, listening to the sound of the breeze through the limbs.

"Alice," he said, not feeling the need to yell. "I know ya can feel me. It's time we had a wee chat."

A cold wind whipped across his back. He felt the rage and hate. If Alice had carried any compassion or happiness, she'd traded it long ago.

Mist gathered over the path, crawling up the trees on either side of him. Alice came forward dressed as a noblewoman from long ago. The red and gold of her gown seemed out of place in the forests of Wisconsin. Her hair was done up like she expected to go to a royal ball.

She carried the kilt he'd left in her cottage bunched in a fist.

"You took something from me." Alice threw the kilt at his feet and placed her hands on her hips. "She was mine. She came to me willingly. You had no right to break into my home and steal from me."

"No person should ever unwillingly belong to another person," Raibeart stated. "Katherine is not yours."

"You think you can keep her from me?" Alice laughed. "Oh, lover, don't you understand? There is nowhere the two of you can go that I won't be able to follow. I always know where you are."

Magick wrapped around Alice's hands, dark and smokey, as it reached for him. It called forth his own powers, the blue of it reaching forward to meet her parasitic need over the dark path.

"Your magick calls to me." Alice stepped toward him. "I heard it in my dreams before we even met. It taunted me with a better life. I knew there had to be more than mucking stalls and fighting off the hands of my mother's latest husband. I knew I had to make a pact, but what did I care if a demon wanted my soul when I was going to have immortality? So I took it, your magick, just as I took you. I should have been enough for you, stupid man, but you wanted her. So I took her. I took your sons. I took your magick and your immortality. I took your sanity. And I can take it all again whenever I want."

"Ya should not have given away your soul. Without it, ya cannot understand the love ya crave." A tiny piece of Raibeart felt sorry for the woman, but only a very tiny, tiny piece. Nothing justified what she had done.

"There is no you without me, Raibeart." Alice grinned.

"I think ya have that wrong." He tried to find something redeemable within her. Her cold rage continued to surround him. Her body pulled at his magick as if desperate to suck every last drop of it from him. "There is no *ya* without *my* magick."

She waved her hand in dismissal. "Say it

however ya want. Doesn't change facts, lover. You are mine."

"Aye, you're right. I can't escape ya or this chain shackling us together." Raibeart reached into the sporran at his waist and pulled out a brass dagger. Jewels encrusted the handle. The weapon had not been used for a long time. It could not be destroyed by man or magick.

"That's very pretty." Alice swept her hand over her hair as if unconcerned. "But it won't kill me."

"It would hurt but aye, you're right, this knife would not kill ya." Raibeart balanced the blade in his palm. "Ya see, this blade is made for killing one thing."

"Katherine?" Alice arched a brow and laughed. "Don't tell me you propose killing your love just to keep her from me? How beautifully tragic."

"I've known without realizing it for a long time. This thing between us, Alice. This path that ya put us on." Raibeart lifted the blade. "This is how a warlock dies."

Raibeart drew the blade down into his chest. He saw the realization dawn on Alice's face. She charged forward to make him stop, but it was too late. The blade entered him, sliding neatly into his heart. The cursed jewels in the handle pulled his magick and sent it back into nature.

Raibeart dropped to the ground, falling onto his back. The pain was nothing compared to the goal it was set to accomplish. This was how it had to be. Katherine would be safe. That is all that mattered.

His one regret was not being able to spend eternity with his sweet Katherine.

The moonlight shone from above between the treetops, reminding him of the nights he'd spent in her arms. It was a memory he would carry with him until the end.

Alice screamed as the ancient dagger stole his magick from within her as well. Without him, there was no open conduit for her to tap. She clutched at the stream of smokey magick, trying to grab hold as it slipped past her desperate fingers.

"Raibeart!" At first, he thought he imagined Katherine's voice screaming his name.

Alice screeched, the ugly cry of her anger hurting his ears.

"Raibeart!" Katherine yelled again.

He turned his head to find Katherine running toward him. Happiness filled him to simply see her face. She was alive, and Alice would never touch her again. He tried to say her name, tried to say he loved her, but no sound came out.

Katherine fell to her knees next to him and grabbed the dagger's hilt.

Alice's screeching stopped.

As Katherine's hands covered the jewels, his magick redirected into her. She yanked the blade from his chest and threw it aside. She pressed her hands to the wound and commanded, "Ya cannot leave me. Ya cannot leave me."

His magick surged from her hands back into him. He gasped as the pain inside him lessened.

"Ya cannot leave me," Katherine repeated, a mix of tears and anger on her determined face.

Raibeart pushed up from the ground, ready to protect her from Alice.

There was no need. Alice lay on the forest path, sculpted in ash. Her figure reached desperately toward him. Her mouth hung open, frozen in her last dying wail.

"Katherine," he managed, his chest tight. "I thought I'd never see ya——"

"What the hell were ya thinking?" Katherine smacked him hard on the shoulder before reaching to kiss him. Her lips pressed into his, moving as if she still wanted to scream at him. When he tried to deepen the kiss, she pulled back and said, "I woke up, and ya were gone. No one could tell me where, but I knew ya were going to do something stupid. I felt it."

"But…" He tried to resume kissing her.

"Ya could have died!" She touched near where he'd stabbed himself.

The bloody cut in the material indicated that he should have.

"What would ya have done if I didn't get here in time?" Katherine's hand shook as she kept her palm flat against his chest. The knife wound in his chest might have healed, but he felt weak from the ordeal.

"How did ya find us?" He leaned to look at the unhealed bite mark on her neck. "Should ya even be out of bed?"

"Should ya be sacrificing yourself in the middle of the forest?" she countered. "I did what ya said. I picked a path and committed, and it took me where I needed to be. It's magick, right?"

He lifted her hand and kissed it. "Our love joins us."

Katherine eyed Alice. "Is she…?"

"Aye." Raibeart stood. He couldn't feel Alice's parasitic pull. His body might ache terribly, but his mind was clear. He'd severed her hold over him.

Raibeart tapped the tip of his boot against her forehead. The gentle movement caused Alice's face to crumble as the ash fell into a pile.

Katherine picked the jeweled dagger off the ground. Raibeart reached out his hand to carry it for her. She held it away from him and shook her head. She ignored his help and stood on her own.

"If we're going to have a future together, no more making decisions without me, Mr. MacGregor," Katherine warned. "And no going off to put yourself in danger. At least not without discussing it with me first."

"Well, future Mrs. MacGregor, I could say the same to ya. No more making decisions without *me*, sacrificing yourself to be imprisoned with bangungot bats because ya think it will keep the family safe. I can't say that was a good idea."

"It wasn't just bats." Katherine gave one last look at the pile of Alice before threading her arm in his and pulling him back toward the house. She leaned into him for support, taking the weight off her ankle. "There was a temperamental unicorn, giant spiders, one of those ocean monsters ya warned me about on the old maps, angry leprechauns that caused the cottage to break apart into a crumbling mess, and these two freaky ghost girls who sang threatening songs about taking away my will to speak."

"Oh, aye, I know the ones. Andras's kids." Raibeart nodded. "We ran across those two hellions before. They're supposed to be burning in the eternal fire with their da."

Katherine glanced back to Alice's ashes and shivered. "So much could have gone wrong."

"It didn't. Fate knew what she was doing. Alice is dead." Raibeart slipped his arm around Katherine's waist. "Forever. For good."

Katherine nodded. "Ya did scare me tonight."

"I meant to save ya," he said. "Death is nothing so long as ya are safe."

"Well, it was stupid. Brave, but stupid."

"Aye. Perhaps." Raibeart scratched his hip. Frowning, he stopped. "One moment, my love."

He pushed the new kilt off his hips and sighed in relief. Then, whistling, he called his enchanted kilt toward him. The material fluttered from where Alice had dropped it on the forest floor. It wrapped itself around his waist.

"Ah, I missed ya, old fella," he told the tattered kilt, petting it along his thigh. "I didn't think I'd see it again."

"Raibeart?" She drew his attention back to her.

"Aye?" He again wrapped his arm around her to support her as they walked over dancing spots of moonlight shining through the trees. The soft breeze caused the leaves to crash overhead.

"Why haven't ya asked me to marry ya?" She

rested her head against his shoulder. "Ya just assumed I was going to be the future Mrs. MacGregor."

At that, he chuckled. "Didn't I ask ya when we first met?"

"No. Ya informed me ya were going to ask my father for my hand in marriage, and he turned ya down."

Raibeart considered her words for a moment. "I've asked that question a million times while searching for ya. I figure ya deserve better, and I respect us too much to question what we have."

"Raibeart? Katherine?" Cait's voice carried over them.

Raibeart stopped. "She sounds upset. Ya want to hide in the forest? I know a spot."

"Raibeart," Murdoch yelled.

"Raibeart!" Angus joined in the search.

"Come on, Raibeart," Margareta ordered. "Enough is enough. Time to come home. Katherine should not be on her feet. She needs rest."

"They're just worried about us," Katherine said. "We should tell them everything is all right."

"Raibeart! Katherine!" Cait called.

"Aye, harpie, relax," Raibeart yelled. "We're here. It's all over."

Katherine paused and took a deep breath. She

used Raibeart for balance as she lifted her ankle. "I tweaked it running to find ya."

"Your chariot, my lady." Raibeart swept her into his arms and began carrying her home. His magick recovered enough that he was able to pull fuel from the trees. It strengthened his walk and allowed him to move faster. When they reached the back gardens, it was to find Gregory and Donovan waiting with Margareta, Cait, Murdoch, and Angus.

"Oh, thank goodness. Ya know it's not safe with Alice on the loose," Cait said. "We need to make a plan. As a family."

Raibeart gently set Katherine on her feet while supporting her so she didn't put weight on her sore ankle.

Margareta frowned when she saw the dagger and snatched it from Katherine's hand. "Where did ya get this?"

"I took it," Raibeart stated. "Don't look at me like that. It is the MacGregor family vault, isn't it? It's not like I stole it."

"I had that safe locked. How did ya get the combination?" Margareta demanded.

"Aye, because it was difficult guessing ya used the date ya met your husband," Raibeart teased. "That's your code for everything."

"We all guessed it years ago," Murdoch admitted.

Cait stepped closer and grabbed Raibeart's shirt. She ripped the torn material wider to look at his chest. "Ya used the dagger?"

"I'm fine." Raibeart swatted her hand away. "My plan worked. Alice is dead. I'm an all-powerful warlock genius."

Gregory and Donovan shared a look at the news.

Katherine pushed away from Raibeart to go to their sons. "I know ya considered her to be your...um."

"We hold no delusion about what she was," Donovan said. "She is not the ma we chose."

"It's honestly hard to believe it's over," Gregory admitted. "We've been cleaning up after her for so long, trying to mitigate her damage."

Katherine lifted her arms to offer them a hug. "I will never be able to thank ya for all ya have done. Or how very proud I am of the men ya have become."

They hesitated before leaning in to accept her affection.

"Ah, there are my boys." Raibeart wrapped his arms around all three of them. "There's a good Dono and Petey Galbraith-MacGregor."

Donovan broke from the hug first. "Any

chance we can crash here for a while? Just until we figure out what we're going to do next?"

"Aye. You're MacGregors," Murdoch said. "It's time ya took your rightful place. You'll stay for as long as ya like. Our home is always your home. When you're ready, we'll set ya up with one of the businesses."

"Raibeart, this conversation is not over." Margareta held the weapon at arm's length and gingerly walked toward the house. "I'm putting this back in the vault. No one else touches it."

"Katherine should be in bed," Cait scolded Raibeart. "Ya should not have involved her in this."

"He tried not to involve me. I went on my own. He's my husband," Katherine stated. "I had to help him. He needed me."

"Your..." Cait looked at Raibeart for confirmation.

"Of course we are married," Katherine smiled at him, wrapping her arms around his neck. "It's a, what is the modern term? Foregone conclusion. We were always going to be married from that first moment. It just took us a little longer than expected to get here."

Murdoch and Angus grinned, taking the news in stride.

"Welcome to the family, sister," Angus said.

"Aye, congratulations," Gregory added. Donovan nodded in agreement with his brother.

Raibeart again swept Katherine into his arms. "Now, excuse us while we go on our honeymoon."

"But ya should come inside. Where are ya going at this hour?" Cait asked.

"We'll know when we get there," Katherine answered.

Raibeart grinned. "What my wife said."

"Let them be, my Cait," Murdoch said. "They're both safe. That's all that matters."

"I just don't understand what happened tonight," Cait told her husband.

"They'll tell us later," Murdoch assured her.

Raibeart strode toward the trees, intent on getting lost with his wife.

When they were alone, Katherine asked, "Hey, why are ya wearing clothes? I thought these midnight runs were supposed to be in the nude."

"Fair enough, wife." He used his magick to melt their clothes away so that they were both naked. The material fell to the ground behind them.

When he reached a wide part of a trail, he whistled for his kilt and directed it to spread onto the ground to make a bed for her.

"Ya heard the orders. Ya need to lie down." Raibeart placed her gently beneath the trees and moonlight. The glow of light on her naked body left him in awe. "Your beauty leaves me breathless. I will spend the rest of my life proving myself worthy of your love."

When he touched her, it felt like heaven. Emotions rushed through him, sparking his magick. All he wanted was to make her happy.

Katherine reached for him, and he obeyed her silent command, leaning over her. Her hands wrapped his neck as if they belonged there. When they touched, it felt as if the centuries faded and no time had passed. Nothing mattered but the moment. His body recognized hers just as his heart beat only her name.

All the messy fragments of his life cleared away when he looked deep into her eyes. She held the lost key to his sanity. All the pieces of his life fit neatly together.

"I have been searching for ya for a very long time," he whispered.

He felt her fingers move, their pressure gliding down his shoulders and back.

"Raibeart," she said his name as if that one word held all their secrets. Nothing more needed to be said because it was understood.

Their relationship had not been a straight line, but even when they couldn't remember each other's faces, that ache to be together had been there. What more was there to life than love? All that was good—empathy, compassion, soul—could be summed up with that one perfect word. Love.

Her kiss only made his hunger for her deepen. His magick surged, wanting to fill her. They did not need words or ceremony to state what had been true for a very long time—their souls were joined. She was always meant to be his wife. He'd known it that first second.

She'd called it a foregone conclusion, but it was more than that. It was a fact—a simple, perfect fact of nature. Just as trees reached for the sun, just as fish swam in the stream, so too did his magick reach for her.

His magick needed her to share in his long life. It wanted to give her everything. And so she would, and so it did.

He knew perfection when he looked down at her spread on top of his kilt. His magick gathered along the bite on her neck to help heal it.

Katherine cupped his naked ass, drawing him into her to end the ache inside them. Raibeart drew his arousal along her sex before thrusting into her completely. She gasped and arched her back. He felt her fevered need and answered the primitive call.

All their fear and longing became desperate

thrusts. Climax came hard in an explosion of love and magick. It poured over into the trees. Wildflowers surged from the surrounding ground, spotting the path with color.

Breathless, she smiled and reached to touch a flower in amazement. "Did ya do that?"

"We did that." Raibeart shifted his weight to rest beside her. He drew his finger along her bottom lip. "When ya saved me with your love, ya took my power and used it. My magick lives inside of ya now. It will only grow with our passing years."

"I feel it." She smiled. "It tickles."

"We're going to do this right. I promise," he swore. "By our sons. By us."

She nodded. A tear slipped down her face. "Aye. No more wasted time. Our sons may be grown, but there is still so much love to give them. They've taken care of us for so long. Now it is our turn."

"Everything I have is yours," Raibeart vowed. "My magick, my life, my heart. It's all yours. Forever. I love ya, Katherine. I always have."

"All I have is my heart," she said, "but it has always belonged to ya."

Chapter Twenty-One

Epilogue

"Does this hurt?" Cait held Katherine's ankle hostage as she checked how the bite was healing. She pressed around the tender tissue.

"Less than this morning." Katherine sat with Cait and Margareta on the front lawn in oversized chairs, watching the streetlights come on in the town below as they drank martinis.

Occasionally a golf ball would fly over their heads as some of the MacGregor men hit them off the roof of the house, including her sons. The second they landed on the ground, the balls disappeared. Margareta had explained that she'd enchanted them, so they returned to their owners. She'd gotten tired of finding them lost in the yard.

The family seemed to be making up for lost time with the twins, often drawing them into their games. For the most part, the grown men appeared fine with the attention until the elders started treating them like lost children. Katherine accepted that their boyhood years had passed, but she was determined to be there for the rest.

Green Vallis had become home. She liked walking through town and exploring each of the buildings. Raibeart knew everyone, and they all seemed to love him, so there was no end to introductions. Well, everyone but the man who owned the pizza restaurant. Apparently, he'd proposed to the man's wife before knowing she was married.

Plus, there was the animal shelter. Whenever she felt overwhelmed, they could go there and soak up the animal magick. That's what Raibeart called it, magick. He meant unconditional love, but it made sense to her.

Katherine felt Raibeart before she heard his footsteps running along the side of the house. She smiled in anticipation.

"I've never seen Raibeart so…" Margareta tilted her head in thought. "Happy."

"Lucid." Cait chuckled. "Sober. He hasn't touched the whiskey."

"Clothed," Margareta added.

Her new sisters-by-marriage laughed as

Katherine held her breath and waited for him to appear. Raibeart sprinted toward them, wearing a puffy bee costume.

Margareta groaned.

Cait gasped. "Oh, for the love of…"

"Bzz, bzz, bzz." Raibeart wiggled his hips before backing toward them with a long, pointed stinger.

"Raibeart Donovan Gregory MacGregor," Cait scolded, swatting at the costume. "Ya cannot wear that into town."

"Bzz?" Raibeart pouted.

"Absolutely not. Put on something fitting this family's reputation." Cait arched a brow and waited.

Raibeart shrugged and waved his hand down his body. His magick glimmered as the bee costume disappeared, leaving him in his kilt. However, since the kilt was draped over his shoulder, it didn't do much to hide his nudity.

"We spoke too soon," Cait said to Margareta. "His mind might be clearer, but he's still the same Raibeart."

Margareta leaned back into her chair and sipped her drink. "Perhaps not exactly the same. It has been nice not having to mesmerize police officers to sneak him out of jail."

"Wife, care for a midnight run?" Raibeart

asked. "The moon lost part of itself, and we should go look."

Katherine glanced up. Only a sliver of the moon shone in the sky.

Cait let go of Katherine's ankle and lifted her hands in defeat. "I had hoped that ya would be a good influence on him, but I see some wild creatures cannot be tamed."

"Why tame perfection?" Katherine grinned.

"At least keep him away from town. Tourist traffic has increased," Cait said. "Maura said the hotel is at ninety-five percent capacity."

"Can't make any promises," Katherine teased with a wink.

"Aye. Will be a hundred and ten percent capacity soon." Raibeart grinned. "I told my internet ladies to come for a visit to meet my wife. Did I forget to mention that we're hosting a party here tomorrow night?"

Cait stiffened. "We're not prepared for a party."

"I have faith in ya, Cait." Raibeart held his hand toward Katherine. "It's only a hundred, maybe three hundred guests. Thousand tops."

"Tell me you're joking," Cait demanded.

Raibeart didn't answer her.

Katherine jogged to meet her husband. When she reached him, she gave a small hop and wrapped her arms around his neck. Her feet dangled off the ground. "Where to tonight, my honeybee?"

Raibeart walked with her hanging from his neck. Her mouth came close to his.

"The possibilities are endless, my love. Let's see where the road takes us," he whispered.

The End

The Series Continues with
Magickal Trouble

The Series Continues

WARLOCKS MACGREGOR® 11: MAGICKAL
TROUBLE

**When warlocks play matchmaker, things
are bound to go wrong.**

Warlock Bruce MacGregor likes his life exactly the
way it is. He has his art, his books, his freedom.
But lately his family has become marriage
obsessed. As one of the last single men standing,
they're all looking at him to find eternal happiness...and they're not above casting a few spells to
ensure it happens.

Magic, Mischief and Kilts!

Warlocks MacGregor® Series

SCOTTISH MAGICKAL WARLOCKS

Love Potions
Spellbound
Stirring Up Trouble
Cauldrons and Confessions
Spirits and Spells
Kisses and Curses
Magick and Mischief
A Dash of Destiny
Night Magick
A Streak of Lightning
Magickal Trouble

More Coming Soon

Visit www.MichellePillow.com for details.

About Michelle M. Pillow

New York Times **& *USA TODAY***
Bestselling Author

Michelle loves to travel and try new things, whether it's a paranormal investigation of an old Vaudeville Theatre or climbing Mayan temples in Belize. She believes life is an adventure fueled by copious amounts of coffee.

Newly relocated to the American South, Michelle is involved in various film and documentary projects with her talented director husband. She is mom to a fantastic artist. And she's managed by a dog and cat who make sure she's meeting her deadlines.

For the most part she can be found wearing pajama pants and working in her office. There may or may not be dancing. It's all part of the creative process.

～

Come say hello! Michelle loves talking with readers on social media!

www.MichellePillow.com

facebook.com/AuthorMichellePillow

twitter.com/michellepillow

instagram.com/michellempillow

bookbub.com/authors/michelle-m-pillow

goodreads.com/Michelle_Pillow

amazon.com/author/michellepillow

youtube.com/michellepillow

pinterest.com/michellepillow

Please Leave a Review

THANK YOU FOR READING!

Please take a moment to share your thoughts by reviewing this book.

∿

Be sure to check out Michelle's other titles at www.MichellePillow.com